S.G. PUBLISHING

URBAN ROYALTY

A BOOG DENIRO **PRODUCTION**

S.G. PUBLISHING
NEW YORK

Urban Royalty is a work of fiction. Any resemblances to real people, or events or locales is merely a coincidence, and purely a product of the author's imagination.

Compilation and Introduction Copyright © 2020
By: S.G. PUBLISHING
Bronx, New York 10453
Email: sgpublishing@gmail.com

ISBN 13:
ISBN 10:
Author: BOOG DENIRO
Cover Design:
Typeset: TySheem Crocker
EDITOR: TySheem Crocker

First Trade Paperback Edition Printing
10 9 8 7 6 5 4 3 2 1
Printed in the USA

ACKNOWLEDGEMENTS

First I'd like to remember my mother, she meant so much to me, and was very instrumental in me becoming the man I am today. *I miss you Regina Crocker*. Rest peacefully mommalove.

Omar & Naquan, I love you both with all my heart. And your children: *Zoey, Zuri, and Zahir*.

Much love to my pop, John Haywood. Much love to my stepfather, Floyd Murray. Both of you have been more than supportive.

Special shout outs to: my little brothers Shondell & Malik, my little sisters Tyasia & Sade!

Shout outs to: Albert Duran, LowLow, Renny, Tankhead Genile, Jemell "Casper" Hill, Rob Weisman, TeeTay, Rock, D.J. Waffles, D.J. Cocoa Chanelle, Khalil Abdul Muhammad, Tiffany, Bay, Prina J., MamaDon, Shalamar, Meka, Takia, Latisha, Tish, Nicky, Dwayne Watkins, Bugatti Bak, Roger "Rabb" Moore, Gary "G-Baby" Boyd, Rah Da Boss, Cassarah Jean, Dontaye "3" Deshields, Country McRae, Brandon Turner, Dennis Boney, Meech Washington, Dame Wall, Brandon Key, Lump, Don Juan, my west homie 1090, OG Knuckles, Basil, Fats, Jacqueline, Roy Galloway, Taronda, my family the Murrays & the Betheas.

BOOG DENIRO

Can't forget my homie Louis Smith, from south Philly. Shouts to my bro China B., Lance Burke, Twin, Chiraq's G. Garmon, Hassan Campbell TV (YouTube), Calvin Posey, Abdul Shakur, Boom Podcast, Team Success, Justice for Youth Foundation, Second Chance Ministries, Charles Pack, Ronnie Austin, Chill Will Pax. *Shouts to my Philly bulls*: Hucklebuck, Mike Bright, Jay St. Talib, Musa "Mir" Hadi, Yasir Gayle, L.B. aka Boo, Big Rich Parker, Mike 'Reem, Ronnie "Unkle" Stone, Du Divine, Zigg Thompson, Tone, Block, Shady Black, V. Vegas, Manny Moch, Wood Rivers, Black Sam, YahYah Black, White Thompkins, G-man Doughty, and all the other real cats I ever did time and/or shared space with. Shouts to all the true and living, the right and exact, living righteous.

RIP to all those we lost; too many to name. In fact, the number of deaths of people I know have quadrupled since the release of my first book 10 years ago. I'd be here all day if I tried to name them all. *Life is short, too short, so live it to the limit when we can*.

Anyone I may've missed, charge it to my mind, not my heart please. Or, you can just write it in yourself, right here: _____.

Always & Forever,

Boog Deniro

INTRODUCTION

JULY 13, 1977
NEW YORK CITY

The city was experiencing a blackout, blanketed in utter and unforeseen darkness. Stores were being looted, properties were being vandalized. And at Lincoln Hospital, in the Bronx, New York, a doctor was delivering a seven pound, 11 inch baby girl. That was the day Angel Harriett Ross was brought into this cold world.

For her first years, all Angel knew was darkness. Well after electricity was restored to the country's most populated city, Angel still lived in dire straits, a home without lights and heat. *Angel was poor.*

By the summer of 1989, she had been exposed to all kinds of violations of the New York penal codes. Unfortunately, crime was a way of life for the impoverished.

Angel was a honey complexion, honey before it is harvested, like her mother. And fully developed by the age of sixteen, just like her mother. Hustlers and heavy hitters all up and down University Avenue, on the west side of the Bronx, wanted to break Angel's fine ass in. She walked with a mean switch, had hair like the Puerto Ricans, eyes like the Asians, and the attitude of a rap star. Angel was Cardi B. before Cardi B. Seductive, tantalizing, outgoing, outspoken, and a stealth learner.

3

When men stared, their eyes would tell her exactly what she was worth. *PRICELESS!* Which meant she would be setting the tone.

The minute Bishop "Bish" King laid eyes on Angel's 5'4", stacked frame, he knew he had to have her. When he heard her talking to his crime partner, it became even more clear—*it didn't matter who he crossed, or how much it would cost, Angel was meant for Bish.*

Their first time alone, Bish got Angel's little fine ass pregnant. The two were truly in love, and took up residence in the city of Brother Love, where Bish was from. They named their firstborn *Mes'siyah King.*

$ $ $

Twenty-two years later, somewhere in Philadelphia, PA, rain poured down from the dark and cloudy overcast skies. Strong winds thrust through the city, making the rain fly sideways. It was just after 5:30 PM, on a Tuesday, so the streets were still very busy. More than enough distractions. But, as I came through in the candy apple red Bentley GT coupe, windows tinted, all eyes were still on me. Everyone wanted to see this distraction. *Yeah, I was heavy.* Bottom line!

I'm Mes'siyah King. Yeah, that Mes'siyah. If you from Philly or New York City, you probably heard of me. My whole life I always knew my dad was a gangsta He'd been running the city for nearly 20 years, with my mother, Angel, by his side. I knew he was next level when he just up and moved us out of southwest, and into this big ass mansion out in Villanova, PA. Eight bedrooms, six baths, a private pool house, built-in theater, an arcade, on 2.5 acres of land. The next closest home to us was a quarter mile down the road.

On the legitimate side of things, my parents owned a popular fashion line called *Dir'Me*. The designers were very creative, so my parents had something for everyone. Women, men, children, suits, rompers, swimsuits, urban, even couture. They even owned a construction company, and a music label. There was also five car dealerships. My folks were paid.

With my pops being who he was, me and my sister, Rubi, were spoiled rotten. I'm used to having it my way, basically doing whatever the fuck I wanted to in these streets. I was getting away with murder. *Literally.* Maybe that's why people say I'm unreasonable sometimes, or egotistical, or narcissistic, and hypersexual???

See, my pops had ties to the Mayor, the District Attorney, both Republicans, whom he donated handsomely to during their campaigns and elections. He had police in pocket, medical surgeons on speed dial, and the new Johnny Cochran on retainer.

The way pops had things running, he had two top dawgs in every part of the city. With the best product in Philly in their hands, they flooded the blocks, bringing back eighty racks off the key. See, that would make the next nine kilos available at $30K. You do the math. *We was heavy.* But it's like the heavier pops got, the less attention pops paid to the streets. A nigga wouldn't dare move in on any of his territories five years ago. But now, with the day and age we were living in, not many controlled blocks anymore. It was 2016, we were in a presidential election year, and most of the hustlers operated off of phones. Hustling off the phone allowed hustlers to go where the money was. And that was in the wrong territory most times.

Now my pops' top dawgs could barely move their loads in a month, when they once dumped them in a week.

I was in the streets! He took me to the suburbs before I was a teen, but he couldn't take me away from 58th Street. I was witnessing the changes, the dares, the double dares. I saw the rebellion coming. And I was there to put an end to it.

See, my dad is 44, and the more legit he became, the less active he was in the streets. Me on the other hand, I could see that it was time for him to step down. So, once I turned eighteen, I got more involved. That was three years ago. You see, I love this gangsta shit, and I was ready to take the thrown. With my gang following my lead, and backing every move I put in play, I was laying down the law. *Straight like that!*

But lately, I been seeing some shit out here in these streets. Niggas was pushing up on my little sister, dudes

6

playing both sides, so I gotta handle that. I ain't got time to be telling my pops shit he can't see, happening right up under his nose. Nah, I'm handle this shit, and answer questions at the funeral. *Period!*

This is *Urban Royalty...*

The Mes'siyah story!

BOOG DENIRO

CHAPTER ONE

APRIL 13, 2016
FRIDAY, 5:30 PM

The Bentley pulled up on 57th and Malcome Streets, and Mes'siyah got out. He ran to the outside porch in some fresh butta Timbos, strings loose and dangling. The black Balmain jeans hugged his legs perfectly. The red belt, gold buckled YSL belt showed, as did the front of this black sweatshirt that read *Dir'Me* in large bold red letters, red stripes going across the chest. The red shiny bubble jacket hung down to his waist, covering the twin shoulder straps containing the gold plated Dessert Eagles.

He adjusted the black *Dir'Me* cap, red logo at center, as the iced out Rolex hugged his wrist, shining and glistening brilliantly. The brightness of the ring on his pinkie demanded just as much attention. Point blank, Mes'siyah had the fashion thing figured out, even more than he had the streets figured out. Celebs were taking tips from him in the city.

After one ring, the door opened. "Wassup, 'Siyah?" Nico said, extending his hand for some skin. Nico was Mes'siyah's right hand man's 16-year-old brother.

"What up, young boy?" Mes'siyah replied, walking into the two story row home.

Checking out Mes'siyah's gear, Nico said, "Chilling. Er'body upstairs, in the back." He shut the door and followed Mes'siyah, mimicking his strut.

"Clearly," Mes'siyah said sarcastically, as he climbed the stairs, two at a time.

"Big bro, can you do me a favor?" Nico asked. Before Mes'siyah could reply, Nico said, "Come get me in the Bentley? From school?"

"Sacari pick you up in the 550, right?"

"Yeah. But, that ain't the Bentley."

Mes'siyah chuckled and continued to move until he got to the bedroom door. "Clearly," he said, as he opened the door, gracing the room with his presence.

Sosa was there. Jack-Jack was present. Cash was lounging. Sauce was in attendance. That was Mes'siyah's immediately circle, all *day-ones*. "Yo, yo, yo! Gang, gang!" Mes'siyah sounded off, giving them all dap. He saved Sacari for last, as he bumped chests with him. There were also a handful of chicks on deck, all looking spectacular.

Sacari walked out the room pulling his hoodie on. Mes'siyah plugged his phones up to the chargers. Nico came in and sat with the gang.

"Nico, get ya lil' ass up out—"

"Hold, chill, let my lil' brah breathe." Mes'siyah stopped them from kicking Nico out.

"Yeah, let me breathe," Nico said, smiling, his cornrows swinging and dangling as Mes'siyah tailed Sacari.

Mes'siyah jogged down the hall lightly, and down the steps even lighter. He exited the front door as Sacari was getting into the passenger seat of the Bentley. Mes'siyah trotted down to the driver's side and got in. He shut the door, leaned back in the butta seat, said, "Dayyyam!"

"What's up?" asked Sacari.

"Us!" They did their 12-combo handshake, like the ones LeBron James did with his teammates before tipoff at a game. "How you though?"

Sacari said, "Same ole G shit."

Sacari was albino. He had blonde hair, every strand on his body, and grayish blue eyes. He had deep, deep rooted waves, and deep dish dimples to go with them. At 5'9", some said he looked scary, some said he was cute. Attracting chicks was not a problem for him.

Mes'siyah had his mother's startling facial features, and his father's height and big beard. Bish was six-foot even, Mes'siyah was 6'1", tall and lanky. He put the fingertips of his left hand on the steering wheel and pulled off. "Who the bitches up there?" he asked.

Sacari said, "Nardia from Summerville. Stars around her nipples. We partied her..."

"In the back of the G-wagon?"

"Nah, the 745. The G-wagon was the bitch GiGi."

"Mermaid tatted on her ass cheek, right?"

"Clearly," Sacari agreed.

They laughed. They'd partied mad bitched together.

The right-hand mans continued to kick it about their many episodes with countless women, from all walks of life, and all parts of Philly, South Jersey, and New York. It's what they did when they were alone, just like most 21-year olds.

"The next bitch we party, you gotta let little bro pop that pussy too," Mes'siyah suggested.

Sacari said, "Nico be trying to love these *thots*..."

"So what? Let him do him. How he gonna learn, if we don't teach him?" asked Mes'siyah as he pulled into the driveway behind 68th and Carroll Streets. They were to meet a local hustler they'd been doing business with over the last year.

"Cool. But why he be trying to eat every bitch pussy? What up with him?" Sacari asked as Mes'siyah laughed, parking the Bentley.

Mes'siyah chuckled as he turned the Bentley off. "I have no idea, but I eat pussy and ass, bro," he said.

They exited the brand new Bentley and made their way up to the back door of the bando. As if on cue, someone knocked on the front door as Mes'siyah stood on the third step looking up. It was Rambo. He peeked out, said, "Wassup?" and Sacari gave him dap, leading Mes'siyah inside. Sacari locked the door behind them with his eyes on Rambo, who was carrying a black Nike duffel that seemed to match his Nike joggers and jacket.

"Who else you grabbing off of, Rambo?" Mes'siyah asked, looking down at his freshly manicured nails.

"These Rican boys from the Boogie Down. They shit better than the shit Bish got. And they two points cheaper," Rambo explained, checking Mes'siyah out.

"So, me, my pops, *aannnd* some Bronx niggahs?" Mes'siyah quizzed, looking back up at Rambo.

"Well, something like that..."

Mes'siyah looked him up and down, real slow and arrogantly. Two days ago, he told Rambo he'd stolen ten kilos from Bish, and was trying to get them off as a startup. Of course, Rambo jumped right on it, confirming to Mes'siyah he was doing something on the side, even though he pledged his allegiance to Bish, the man who put Rambo on when Rambo was only fifteen.

"What you grade out shit?" Mes'siyah asked.

Rambo said, "A strong B-plus."

"And them?"

"*A-plus!* Numb everything down to the back of ya neck, on the gum test," Rambo explained, rubbing his belly which was protruding from his jacket.

Mes'siyah looked shocked. It was at that point that the *Son of Bishop* thing really kicked in. Mes'siyah wanted badly to be just like his pops.

See, Rambo knew all too well that Mes'siyah knew all the young up-and-coming players in the city. Not to mention, all the move-makers 35 and older. Seeing how Bish managed to run the city for nearly twenty straight years, with consistent B-grade product, Rambo knew what Mes'siyah could do with some raw shit. He could see Mes'siyah running things with the top notch connect he now had. For Rambo, that wouldn't be good for *B.I.*

"Nah, see, they only dealing with a chosen few," Rambo said, shrugging his shoulders.

"Come on bro, link me in. Line me up," Mes'siyah requested, walking into the back room.

A plastic sheet that painters would use covered off half the room. Plastic was taped down on the floors and some of the walls. Sacari pulled the Glock 20 off his hip and walked in behind Mes'siyah.

Rambo hit a throwback Beanie Segal lyric,"*I ain't the captain of the yacht, I'm just on the boat.*"

Mes'siyah was pulling on a Newport from the box. The only cigarettes he smoked. Rambo looked around. He was only 22-years old, but he'd been around, seen a lot with those young eyes. Somebody was about to die. He just didn't think he'd been setup. He seen the body bag, and panic quickly settled in. Mes'siyah put a flame to his Newport and puffed, lifting his head.

"Sorry to hear that," he said, lungs full of smoke.

Rambo reached for his piece, but it was too late. *BOACK! BOACK!* The loud 10-mili Glock made Rambo's brains explode like a pipe bomb. Rambo's fat ass hit the plastic like a ton of bricks. Mes'siyah puffed his *cig* while Sacari stood over Rambo. *BOACK!* Three to the head.

"Okay, let's get to work," Mes'siyah said.

With latex gloves on, they wrapped his body in the thick plastic and duct tape, then put the body into the body bag. Sacari snatched the plastic off the wall, exposing the hole in it. Mes'siyah grabbed the nail gun. They put the body in the wall, and nailed it to the wall's

14

pillars so it stayed up. They nailed the drywall over the body bag, and no one could even tell it was there. They snatched up Rambo's car keys, iPhone and duffel, and headed out the same way they'd come in.

"Time?"

"*Fourteen* minutes..." Sacari said.

"Not bad." Mes'siyah turned the corner, flicking the Newport out the window, as the rain began to slow up. He tossed the phone out the window, doing about 60 mph, making sure it would break into pieces.

They pulled back to the curbside near Sacari's mother's house with $250,000 in the back seat. 5:55 PM! They were back before anyone even knew they had left. Sacari tossed the hoodie on the chair and pulled off his T-shirt, revealing his pale but super tatted physique.

Everyone was laughing and chatting, smoking and joking. Nico was sandwiched between a curvy 20-year old named Heaven, and a nubile beauty named Elle. Sacari stood in front of Heaven, unbuckling his Gucci belt. Heaven looked up at him as her girls got quiet. Every last one of the females on the premises were of age, and promiscuous, but had never been around dudes like Mes'siyah and Sacari.

Mes'siyah sat, leaning back, in this red lounge chair, swiping the screen on his phone. Sacari pulled his dick out, and gently grabbed the back of Heaven's head, right below her long raven ponytail. Heaven looked around at her girls whom all held curious stares. Not one uttered a word, as Sacari guided her glossy and ripe and juicy lips to his to his growing penis. And as if they'd practiced this lewd act, Heaven opened her mouth letting Sacari in. Mes'siyah scrolled through Instagram, thinking nothing of it, while all the others present looked on intrigued, or covered their eyes. What they didn't know was, ...Heaven had actually dared Sacari to pull out on her in front of everyone. *Money was also involved.*

Within minutes, all the bros were getting fellatio, even Nico's young ass. Well, all except Mes'siyah. He only went for the *baddies*. It was a privilege for a girl to even be seen with him. Not to mention, he was super cocky. Sometimes to a fault.

Bish called Mes'siyah's phone, so he left the orgy.

"What up, old head?"

"What's going on, young boy?" Bish replied.

Mes'siyah repeated, "What's going on?"

That's when he heard his mother's voice. He said, "Ma, how you doing? I watered your plants this morning before I rolled out."

"*Clearly*, Mes'siyah," Angel said, having added her son's lexicon to her lingo. "You used too much water."

"We need to talk," Bish said, cutting in.

"OK. Holla at me when you get in. I'll be up waiting," said Bish, pulling Angel across their Cali King bed, and into his waiting arms.

LATER THAT NIGHT, Mes'siyah pulled up to the gates at 2 AM. As the gates locked behind the GT coupe, Mes'siyah came down the long driveway and pulled around the huge stone water fountain made into the shape of a *king* sitting on a befitting throne. He park between the Rolls Royce and the Porsche Cayman. He got out and stood on the oval driveway. Two chess style books, made out of stone, sat at the bottom of the steps. Then a knight was on the ledge of the stone railing. A bishop was up against the wall beside the large dual opened maple wood doors. **King & Queen** was engraved in the glass portion of the doors.

Mes'siyah walked into the house, pure elegance filling his eyes. He made his way to the oval office, behind the kitchen. Bish had a large bookshelf, which no one knew about, except he and Mes'siyah. The secret door lead to a secret lower level that wasn't on the blueprint of the house. Mes'siyah opened the door, and walked into the secret passage that lead to a room full of cash, safes, TV monitors, body armor, assault rifles with bump stocks, and all those B-grade kilos.

Mes'siyah sat at the desk in the large throne style chair. He called his dad. While waiting on Bish's arrival, Mes'siyah brought his sister's room into view. There were cameras and audio monitors all over the mansion that only Bish, Angel and Mes'siyah knew about. Not much, if anything, got pass the man of the mansion. They also had a motion sensor alarm system, and an ex-marine leading the security duty.

It was late, but Rubi King was still up, on her phone, talking. Rubi was eighteen, had just graduated from charter school in June of 2015. Rubi could be naïve at times, but if she was telling it, she'd say *"I'm just a bit misunderstood."*

"Bitch," Rubi said, laughing. "Yessss! I just got in. He was all over me." Rubi smiled, palm smacking her thigh, before her hand went to her curly locks and she twirled. "I dropped him off."

As far as features, Rubi would put you in the mind of the *Boo'd up* singer Ella Mai. Rubi was just thicker.

Mes'siyah heard Bish enter the office, and turned the audio off, while exiting out, leaving their *Dir'Me* logo as the screen saver. He knew Bish would have a fit if he knew Mes'siyah was spying on his precious Rubi. When she turned eighteen, Rubi made it clear, she was grown now.

Mes'siyah turned the chair towards the entrance door, and Bish walked in rocking a black silk robe with matching pants, no shirt on. Silk slippers were on his size eleven feet, and the Presidential Rolex was on his left wrist. *Yes*, even at two in the morning, Bish kept time in style.

Bish said, "I wanna give you the keys to the city." His hands were in his robe pockets as he looked down on his firstborn. "But, I gotta see that you can handle it. Your cousin got some things going on, on the west side of the Bronx. I want you to handle things with him. If you can manage that, I'ma send you more to oversee for us, Mes'siyah."

"Auntie RiRi's son, Mally Gz, right?"Bish said, "Yes, ya momma's sister RiRi's son...Mally Gz."

A man from his past with a similar name came to mind.

"Cool."

Bish said, "I got too much to focus on, and still run the city. You got a year to show me you're ready and you can handle things effectively."

"Clearly."

"We ain't thugs, son. We are gangsters. We ain't shooting up the city when cats owe us, we make"—Bish took his hand from his right pocket, and blew into the air, acting as if that gust was enough to move his hand—"*vanish.*"

"Clearly," Mes'siyah said, smiling and stroking his thick dark beard.

"But, if you can't handle it, I'ma give the keys to Whispers." Whispers was Bish's right-hand man, a brother he came into the game with.

"I got this," Mes'siyah said, sitting up from his lounging position, and rendering his undivided attention.

"Believing is seeing," Bish said, then exited as fast as he had come. His Angel was waiting on him.

Mes'siyah smiled as he rotated the throne back to the monitors. "Hmmm...he know wassup. I been running this shit though. Now I just got an official title," slightly escaped Mes'siyah's mouth. He was determined to make his father proud. Then he got back to eavesdropping on Rubi...

"No, I ain't fuck him..." Rubi said, still twirling her tresses. "His dick is big though. Like seven, eight inches." Rubi batted her lashes, blushing and yawning at the same time. "I did let him taste my pussy though. He kept begging me, so I obliged him..."

Mes'siyah listened and watched, wondering who he was going to have to make disappear next...

CHAPTER TWO

APRIL 17, 2016
TUESDAY, 1:04 PM

Mes'siyah got out the Bentley on 54th and Florance, slamming the door with the sun kissing his skin. It was like he always needed attention, validation of some sort. A major dice game was going on against the concrete wall, in front of one of the bandos.

Rico Havoc, an up and coming local MC, was out there with his gang. Stickup dudes, dope boys, pill poppers, and syrup heads were also scattered about taking in the scene. The ages ranged from sixteen up to mid-twenties, a mix of both genders. About 35 to 40 in total filled the block. And they all knew each other.

Chicks, cars, clothes and jewels were on full display. Mes'siyah fit right in. *As a matter of fact, he stuck out.* Two gold links hung from his neck, dangling just below his collarbone. The 58th STREET medallion and chain with diamonds all over it was longer. When his hand went up to *high five* Sacari, the gold Rolex with the baguette bezel elevated him above all. Sacari was shining too though. So was the rest of their squad.

Sosa, Jack-Jack, and Cash gave Mes'siyah some love while everyone stopped what they were doing to steal of peek of the rising star. He couldn't contain his smile, he was still reeling from the 2 AM convo with Bish.

Mes'siyah went to Instagram Live, holding his phone

21

as he placed his arm around Sacari and said, "Dis how da block look when da top dawgs wanna enjoy a 85 degree day. His first day back in the city!"

"Clearly!" Sacari cosigned.

"Dis dat 58th Street love, baby!" Sosa added.

"You only get this out southwesss!" Cash explained, making sure his chains were sitting on his chest properly. And they were. *All three.*

"Clearly!" Jack-Jack joined in saying.

Everywhere Mes'siyah went he was shown love. From the dirt bike boys, the cats on the 4-wheelers, to the chicks jockeying for position. He felt like Mitch without Rico. *Paid In Full.*

Hours quickly passed, and Mes'siyah was ready to put that scene behind him. Then he heard a familiar voice bickering at the fading dice game. Bankroll and RaRa were at each other's throats again. Mes'siyah knew a day would come when one had killed the other. He stepped in between them when he peeped RaRa reaching for his waistline.

"Relax," Mes'siyah urged, grabbing RaRa's wrist.

Everyone knew if he pulled it, RaRa used it. RaRa was 5'2" with a mean Napoleon complex. Mes'siyah whispered in RaRa's ear, "Everybody looking. You're going to State Road. Chill."

Slowly nodding his head, RaRa bit his bottom lips. Mes'siyah nodded back. Then, their palms met. With Bankroll under his wing now, he further defused things by walking him away. Sacari and Sosa watched closely.

When the two hit the corner, Mes'siyah noticed two

cops on foot patrol, so he leaned on the hood of his car. Once everyone was alerted to the presence of police, Mes'siyah told Bankroll, "Just 'cause you getting money don't mean you can't get shot."

"I'm strapped too." He had an automatic with a ladder sticking out the waistline of his skinny jeans.

"Listen, it's better to have friends than enemies."

Bankroll looked at Mes'siyah like he was crazy. He knew Mes'siyah didn't let things slide. And had the roles been reversed, no one could talk Mes'siyah down. On top of that, he knew Mes'siyah was only protecting his own interests, at the end of the day.

"Mes'siyah King," the burlier of the two cops said, as they moved along checking things out.

"Enjoying the weather, that's it," Mes'siyah said, making eye contact with them both.

"That's good. That's what we want to hear," the thinner lawman said, causing Bankroll to suck his teeth.

Mes'siyah watched them until they were back in their cruiser. He watched until they pulled off. After that he told Bankroll it would be good for the hood if he gave RaRa back some of the money he lost gambling.

Bankroll took the advice, returning RaRa $1,000. And all was good again. Mes'siyah was glad he was able to intervene. And as he was grinning inside, a white 911 Porsche with the top down pulled up. A white 325i pulled up. A 500 SL too. And then a black Range Rover 4.3. Mes'siyah watched from a distance.

What the fuck...thought Mes'siyah....*All dames behind the wheels.*

Turned out the young women, appearing to all be in their early twenties, and enjoying the fruits of life, already knew Sosa's pretty boy ass. Even if Sosa wasn't on Mes'siyah's team, he would've been good. His pops was working with farms of weed back in Kingston, Jamaica. They called him Big Dread.

"Hey, daddy," the driver of the convertible Porsche cooed to Sosa. She stood a little over five foot, was a honey glazed complexion, and her attire left very little to the imagination. "I seen you on *IG Live*, so I figured I slide through, you and your gang; me my girls."

She had come ten deep, and all *baddies*. None of them appeared to need a sponsor. In fact, they were either in college, or a trust fund baby.

Styling his Gucci outfit and kicks, Sosa pulled her to him and kissed her passionately.

Sacari whispered something to Mes'siyah that made him smile. After enjoying some of Sosa's lips and tongue, Ms. Porsche said, "Mini, Littles, Winter, Ivory, Brooklyn, Gigi, Kat, Heather, Nafisah...y'all already know my dude. Meet his friends..."

Sosa said, "Meet Mes'siyah, Sacari, Jack-Jack, and Cashis."

"King Mes'siyah, that is," Mes'siyah interjected, with his hand extended for Ivory's.

His boys were surprised he didn't stay bossed up and texting, like he normally did when they met knew new woman.

As Ivory's soft hand entered his, Littles offered, "I'm Littles and this is my twin Mini..."

Mes'siyah paid Littles and her twin sister very little mind. All his attention belonged the five-foot-three beauty standing in her gladiator style Versace sandals. Her pink French pedicure toes were the prettiest he'd ever seen. Her *slim thick* frame put his eyes in a maze without a map.

She wore a tan Versace romper that stopped right under her plump butt cheeks, with a plunging neckline that went all the way down to her waistline. Her chest and slight cleavage showed because her perky breasts had no bra. No stomach, thirty inches of ass and hips all looked right on her.

Mes'siyah licked his lips, as he put his phone in his pocket. Ivory's neck, wrist, ears and right ankle had diamonds. Mes'siyah immediately checked the fourth finger of her left hand to see if she was engaged or married. Her blonde hair came down to her back. It was straight with the baby hairs laid down on her forehead and temples. Her nails were done just like her pedicure. Mes'siyah zoned in on her pink and pouty Kylie Jenner lips, then the rest of her makeup. She had on eyeliner and a smoky shadow, complementing her long lashes. Her brows had the perfect arch, and set off her crystal blue eyes.

Yeah, Ivory was a white girl, and the only one amongst her circle, looking like that *E! TV* reality show work. And yes, she had Mes'siyah's conceited ass momentarily mesmerized. Only the sound of someone calling his name snapped him out of it.

"King Mes'siyah, I'm Ivory Manning…"

The Manning name rang a bell. And not because of Peyton and Eli Manning. But at that moment, it wasn't important.

Littles had the whole diva shit on smash, and thought she looked *waaaay* better than Ivory, so she continued to give her cat eyes and attention to the boss.

"You know who my father is?" asked Ivory, her right hand still nestled in Mes'siyah's.

Mes'siyah and the gang laughed. None of that mattered to them. *Fathers, mothers, brothers, boy-friends.* None of that shit mattered. If anything smelled funny, they were deading it, then stuffing the body in the wall. Just like in *THE WIRE.*

Ivory looked Mes'siyah up and down, looking for a flaw, a blemish, a weakness, something he may've been insecure about. He wasn't muscular like the guys she normally went for. Other than that she couldn't find one thing to not like about his cocky ass. He took a call, one that demanded his immediate attention. At the con-clusion, he said to Ivory, "I gotta go, but I'll be back by nine. Ocean Palms!"

"I know the place," Ivory replied, nodding in agreement.

He eyed Ivory down as he walked around to the driver's side. "Make sure you there," he said.

Sacari got up, and the Bentley pulled off with YOUNG MA playing, and Mini, Littles, and Kat eyeing intently. They all wanted the Mes'siyah.

26

CHAPTER THREE

Later that night, Mes'siyah got out the Bentley at Ocean Palms, a luxurious 5-star restaurant, where he was to meet his squad and the girls. His cousin on his father's side, Big Body, happened to have the door. He was a 6'7", 280 lbs bouncer, all muscle, and a few years older than Mes'siyah.

Upon seeing Mes'siyah, Big Body dapped him up and hugged him at the same time. Big Body wasn't about the street life. But he did like that fast money, the fast women, and nice things. Knowing his bloodline had things on smash constantly invaded his thoughts. As he watched Mes'siyah disappear into the busy restaurant, Big Body looked up at the star filled sky and decided to ask for a little help. Just something to put a little extra cheese in his pocket.

Inside, Mes'siyah made his way to the ocean view seats reserved for him. There his squad was, laughing and joking. He noticed a few individuals he wouldn't normally convene with on the scene. He gave all his boys some dap, then chucked the deuce at the accompanying females. He immediately noticed that his boys were all coupled up, and that Ivory wasn't present. So he put a chair between the twins, Mini and Littles. Mini smiled, and Littles leaned up to whisper something in Mes'siyah's ear.

He whispered back, "Where is Ivory Manning? If she

doesn't show up, we can slide off..."

Littles and Mini were both cute and appealing, but he wanted to ravish Ivory.

Sacari had placed everyone's orders already. He knew what Mes'siyah liked to eat and drink. As they waited, dudes walking by greeted and shook hands with Mes'siyah, further increasing Littles' intrigue in him. She slipped her hand in his lap, under the table making, Mes'siyah jump. This mixed race, half-black half-white minx was brimming with maneuvers like that.

Mes'siyah smiled, thinking, *life is good*.

The steaks, the shrimp, the lobster tails, the drinks just kept coming, as did Littles' flirtatious behavior. The king was loving it.

He was stuffing his face when Danny Garcia, Meek Mill, and Sevyn Streeter, and Ms. Milano came by their table. They all respected Mes'siyah and the King family name, so they spoke to Mes'siyah. He was almost inebriated off the Hennessey White, so he kept all interactions rather brief. He needed all his energy for what was happening at his happening table. And then, in ambled Ivory Manning.

Littles and Mes'siyah noticed her at the same time.

Ivory had changed clothes, handbags, jewelry, and her hairstyle. She looked even better than she did the first time Mes'siyah laid eyes on her.

Mes'siyah left his seat and pulled the extra chair for Ivory. He squeezed it between Mini and himself, and had Ivory on one side and Littles on the other.

"Your consin, *Big Body King*, said don't forget about

him."

Mes'siyah said, "I know who your father is. *Sydney Manning.*"

"And, apparently he knows who you are."

"Clearly. I have his number too."

Ivory's brows furrowed, as she could smell the liquor on Mes'siyah's breath. She liked the aroma. *How am I going to romance this gangster if he knows my father?* She was hoping he was playing. But, he wasn't. He pulled the number up on his iPhone, showed it to her.

While she was contemplating, he ordered her some grub and a non-alcohol beverage.

"I wanna get tipsy too," she whispered to Mes'siyah as the waitress was about to walk away.

"Mes'siyah said, "Another bottle of Dom too!"

Ivory leaned over and was about to say something to Mini when her phone buzzed. Ivory answered the unknown number, and it was Mes'siyah saying, "You killing that Chanel wrap-around and them open-toe pumps. I love pretty toes. And the titties is sitting up and kissing and all that."

"You have my number too?" she quizzed while at the same time flattered by Mes'siyah's ability to express what he liked about her.

"I get whatever I want," he said.

Ivory was about to reply when an athletic built fellow walked by with his pale skin super tanned. He did a double-take, then an once-over.

"Ivory Manny?" he said.

"Trevor McCarthy?" she shot back.

Before Trevor McCarthy could say another word, Ivory corrected him. "And the family name is *Manning*, like the first family of the NFL, not *Manny*..."

Mes'siyah was feeling Ivory's spunk, and let it be known with a simple smile of approval.

Trevor McCarthy was a star linebacker at Penn State University, and projected to go in the first round of the 2017 NFL draft. He knew Ivory from high school. And he also knew her family very well, which is why Trevor said, "What are you doing with these *people*?"

"These *people*? What is that supposed to mean?" asked Mes'siyah. Although his father ran a crime family for most of his life, Mes'siyah had grown up privileged too. He'd been to social gatherings, and heard people whisper things like that behind his father's back. So he knew exactly what Trevor was alluding to.

Mes'siyah stood. "Who's ya father? He never taught you to speak when spoken to? Ya moms, she never told you—say excuse me—when a grown man is talking? Better question! *Who the fuck are you*?"

Playing organized sports for most of his life, Trevor had interacted with kids from all walks of life. So he knew the guys Ivory was sitting with were bad news. It had nothing to do with race or culture, and everything to do with creed.

Ivory knew this and began looking for a way to defuse this situation. "Mes'siyah, stop please," she said, latching on to the arm holding his Rolex.

"What the hell did you just say?" Trevor said, seething and pinching the bridge of his nose.

All other communication ceased at the table.

"You heard what I said," replied Mes'siyah, shooing the 260 pound defensive linebacker.

There was no doubt in Trevor's mind he could crush Mes'siyah in a fist fight. But he wanted no parts of the young men rising up and surrounding Mes'siyah like he was a god.

Mes'siyah took a sip of the Henny White, and as he was sitting his glass down, Big Body was trekking over. He hadn't taken his eyes off of his little cousin the entire night.

"What up, Family?" Big Body said, all hype.

"Bozo here acting crazy. Using belittling words to describe *important people*. He probably thinks *we ain't got nothing to lose*, like Donald Trump famously said."

"*What?*" the linebacker said. "I was concerned about a friend. Not even thinking about race," he added, looking around to see who was paying attention, and maybe videoing the messy interaction. No one was. Too busy enjoying themselves. *Good*, he thought.

Big Body said, "Let's go." Trevor was no stranger to Ocean Palms, so Big Body was very respectful. Just did his job. Trevor complied, because the last thing he wanted was for his draft stock to drop over a bitch who had been playing hard to get since he'd known her.

Ivory's heart was racing. And it didn't seem to slow down until she was in her car, on the freeway, and on the asphalt of her family's driveway. Never before had she met a guy more cocky, or one with such a personality who knew her father personally...

BOOG DENIRO

CHAPTER FOUR

APRIL 24, 2016
TUESDAY, 7:04 AM

Jamal Ross grew up with his aunt Angel being his favorite person in the whole wide world. She was beautiful, smart, fashionable, and kept a buck in her purse during a time when the Ross family was ensnared in poverty. Angel was his mother's only sibling.

Jamal Ross was now going by Mally Gz, and running things up on Macombs Road, a Bronx, New York, block about a mile from Yankee Stadium. His Auntie Angel tossed him a brick a few years back, and Mally Gz never looked back.

The Rosses weren't the Kings of New York, but they were doing damn good now.

Mally Gz still lived in the neighborhood he grew up in, and on this particular morning, he was up rubbing his pregnant girlfriend's feet while waiting on a call from his cousin Mes'siyah...

Meanwhile, back in Philly, the linebacker Trevor was being escorted into the office of Sydney Manning, after several unsuccessful attempts over the past week. He couldn't wait to tell Manning what had transpired in Ocean Palms.

"Go ahead in. Mr. Manning will see you now," Trevor was told by a smiling and nimble woman.

33

"Trevor, I understand you have some information for me," Manning said. "Have a seat. And this better be good, young man."

"Yes, yes sir. I do," Trevor said, as he unfastened the two buttons of his tweed sports jacket, before sitting. "Well, ya see, I was out last week, and I ran into Ivory. She, and her friends, were seated with a bunch of gang bangers."

Manning looked up and over the designer frames sitting cozy atop the bridge of his pointy nose. "My Ivory?" he asked, staring sternly. "What did they look like?"

Trevor cleared his throat, before saying, "After asking around the next day, I was able to find out that his name is…Mes'siyah, Mr. District Attorney."

$ $ $

Mes'siyah's phone rang for the umpteenth time straight. He sighed as he opened his eyes, reaching for the nightstand. He grabbed his phones and answered the wrong one. *Hello, shit...*" He switched phones, brows and lashes tight, eyes low and barely open. "Yeah, what's up?" he said, finally answering the right phone. The *Money Making Mitch* album could be heard playing in the background.

"Yo, what's shaking Bee? What's good, Fam? You up, my guy?" Mally Gz said, looking out the six story window of his Bronx, New York apartment.

"Dawgs, it's only eight o'clock," Mes'siyah replied,

34

pulling a huge pillow over his face. "And quit with all that New York lingo."

"Come on, you know you jacking the swagg, Bee. Ya moms is originally from N.Y. Where you think she get all that swagg from?"

The two cousins laughed. Mes'siyah could not front, there wasn't a woman flier than his mother. Not in Hollywood; not in the hood.

"You still sleep?" Mally Gz asked.

"Clearly."

"Come on, sun. You know...*the money never sleep.*"

"How much we talking?"

"$250,000..."

Mes'siyah said, "I'm up now."

"Bring the wave. I got a gang of goonies waiting on me. So, they can do they numbers. You dig???"

"I'll be there by noon."

"Say less, my G. And don't forget, my swagg on a mafucking bean! You heard?"

They shared another laugh, talked a bit more about their mothers, then Mes'siyah dialed Bish.

"Young buck, you up early?"

"The money never sleep," Mes'siyah replied, jacking his cousin's swagg.

"Clearly," Bish said, jacking his son's swagg.

"Mally is ready."

Bish said, "Already?"

"That's what he said."

"Alright. You know what to do."

Mes'siyah said, "Clearly," then hung up.

Mes'siyah got out of bed and slowly stretched. He strolled into his walk-in closet, and took about 30 minutes to decide what he would wear. Another hour went into his daily hygiene. Once he was dressed, jewels on, he made his way over to Rubi's room which was on the other side of the mansion.

Rubi was sleeping like the princess she was. He opened the cream embroidered curtains, letting the bright sunrays in, then snatched the creamy silk sheets from over Rubi's face.

She knew no one else on the face of the earth would do such a thing, so without even opening her hazel eyes, she shouted, "Mes'siyah!" then reached out and hit the intercom button. "Mooooommmmm! He's messing with me again…"

"Siyah, leave her alone," Angel replied.

Angel was already up. She rose with the sun every morning. This day was no different.

"Oh, we telling now? Let's tell mommy how you ain't get in til three, a couple days ago. Four, a couple weeks ago. Tell her about the nigga you driving around in ya Porsche truck."

Rubi's eyes popped open. She was shocked that Mes'siyah knew her most intimate business. No question, her father and brother were well connected, but she swore no one saw her out and about, doing her thing, just experiencing life's trappings.

"That's what I thought," Mes'siyah said, smiling. "You gonna get a nigga smoked, you keep playing with me. And they never find the body. *Understand?*"

36

"*Clearly!*" Rubi said out the side of her mouth, then rolled her eyes wild hard. She adored her big brother, but there were times when she just couldn't stand him, and wished ungodly things for him.

Mes'siyah grinned, tossing the covers on the plush carpet before letting himself out. Fuming, Rubi sat up. And just as she did, Mes'siyah was doubling back. He said, "Oh, how many times you think a nigga gonna let you convince him to eat that *twat* without you returning the favor? You having to put out?"

"*What???*"

"Before he say *fuck it, fuck you, fuck ya family*, and take the pussy???"

He didn't give Rubi a chance to respond. He just shut the door behind him, leaving her there baffled.

Angel was at their super long island that sat up to twenty people, separating their main from the stat-of-the-art kitchen, when Mes'siyah reached the main landing. A continental breakfast, prepared by a renown chef, had just been particularly placed for his beloved mother. She was sitting alone. Just her, the food, and the Daily News.

"Hey, baby boy. Eating breakfast with me?" she asked, as Mes'siyah kissed her cheek.

"Sorry, but I can't," he said, picking up a strip of her bacon. He scooped a pancake and some eggs too.

"If you're not eating with me, go on," she suggested, shooing him at the same time.

"He poured a little sweet maple syrup on the stolen morsels, then took a sip of Angel's fresh squeezed OJ, while her sharp eyes scanned the newspaper.

"I love you, ma," Mes'siyah said. "I'm heading up to *your* old neighborhood."

Angel looked up and rolled her eyes, but also smiled. Mes'siyah was her young prince, and he could do nothing to fuck that up. She spoiled him more than she did Rubi, and she knew it, but would never openly admit it.

Angel got pregnant with Mes'siyah in New York when she was seventeen, and just figuring out what her purpose in life was. He made her grow up fast, made her think big, made her leave New York so she could give him a better life.

Angel said, "I'll be here when you get back. If you see my sister, tell her my number hasn't changed."

Mes'siyah grabbed the bag containing the kilos, and was gone. He reached New York in less than 2 hours.

He met up with Mally Gz, and they got straight to business. In one of Mally Gz's many stash houses, they tallied the money, and negotiated a fair fee for the bricks Mally Gz would be taking on consignment. Mally Gz had been getting other offers, he was doing his thing so hard, so it was important the numbers made sense even if the Kings were family. After all, Mes'siyah was in charge now.

"I think, in this climate twenty-eight is more than fair," Mally Gz said, smoothing out the pant legs of his fresh Nike joggers that matched his Foam Posits. He was also wearing a Cuban link with the Jesus piece like the late Big Poppa used to wear.

They shook on it, then went to Harlem for a New York favorite—*Chopped Cheese*. They washed them down with ice cold lemonade.

Before getting back on the Interstate, Mes'siyah scooped up the money bags Mally Gz owed his parents. Right before he crossed the Ben Franklin Bridge, his phone rang. He noticed it was Ivory. They hadn't spoken since the night at the Ocean Palms.

"What up?" he said, changing lanes. The phone went silent, and he had to check to make sure she was still there. "*Ivory??? With ya lil sexy ass...*"

"You know, my dad never wanted me seeing the bad boy type. Then here you come, and not only does he talk to you, but he gives you my number."

"*Mmmm...*"

"The guys my dad picks for me are usually nerds, guys who play golf, clean cut dudes."

"And you're telling me this why?"

"He sees no problem with me seeing you."

"That's because I'm different. *Clearly.*"

"Who are you?" Ivory asked.

"Who am I?" Mes'siyah said, dipping in and out of lanes like he didn't have a trunk full of money. "Me..."

Ivory waited a minute, then said, "I know there's more to you than what you put on display..."

"Who am I? *Mes'siyah King.* Angel and Bishop's only son. I come from wealth. My moms and pops turned nothing into something. And, I'm next up."

"Interesting."

"Clearly. I'm about my business. The flyest brother

in the mutha-fuking Nation, and beyond," he said, checking the rear view.

"As in the United State, Mes'siyah?"

"Clearly."

Ivory laughed. She thought that was cute. She also thought it was a lot more to the King Family than her father was letting up on. District Attorney Manning was usually loquacious. But not concerning the Kings.

"So what up, you wanna be my main jawn?"

He was used getting anything he wanted, any woman he wanted. And he was used to having more than one at a time. After asking around, Ivory knew this too. Yet, she still said, "Yeah. I wanna be ya main jawn."

"Clearly..."

Ivory Manning giggled, then hung up before she changed her mind.

Mes'siyah was pulling up to the gates, and they were opening for him, so he never took his foot off the gas.

Inside, he put the family money in the vault, and kept his cut in his pocket. Even though his mother was in the mansion too, he called her.

"Hey, my young prince," Angel cooed.

"You got some time for the handsome king-to-be?" he asked, making his way to the second floor. "I'm on my way to my room."

"You're back already?"

"Facts."

Not even a minute later, Mes'siyah was walking into the huge walk-in closet. He had hundreds of sneakers and boots, beside a couple dozen pairs of hard bottoms.

He had a pair from every fashion designer with a household name. He glanced back over his shoulder before entering his small vault. It was a gift from Angel for his eighteenth birthday.

After hitting the combination, it popped open. Stacks upon stacks of neatly unfolded mitts stared back at him. He sat the money he'd made that day in New York inside, then pushed it shut.

Mes'siyah was a neat freak, and only one of the four maids was allowed in his room. He cleaned his room himself, and everything was always strategically placed. That way he could tell if someone was in his room.

He took a quick shower, and freshened up, changing clothes shortly after. That's when he noticed something was out of place. Someone had touched his bed, and he could tell by the ripples in the sheets. He pressed the intercom, said, "Ma, you ready?"

"Yeah, just putting my stilettos on," Angel said, strapping her strappy sandals to her ankles and defined calves.

"Alright. Penelope, lemme get ya ear for a sec' too."

Penelope said, "Just a minute."

Penelope was about to turn thirty, and had been working for the Kings for seven years. She had come to America with a caravan, crossing the border, when she was twelve, been in the U.S. since, and made good money keeping the King compound nice and clean. The first time Mes'siyah saw her in his home, his manhood became erect. That's how attractive Penelope was then.

She was even more beautiful now. Especially in her maids uniform. She was able to dress down on the weekends, and did a damn good job in the fashion department too.

Mes'siyah opened the door to his bedroom, and leaned against the wall, waiting for her, as Sacari called his phone. "Yo, gang."

"Fuck you at?" asked Sacari.

"Was in the Rotten Apple, visiting family."

"We waiting on the *King*. You coming through?"

"Got a date with moms. Once a week thing."

Penelope was coming towards Mes'siyah in her baby-doll shoes, white satin ruffled socks, black miniskirt, and tight white short sleeved button down shirt with the top two buttons open. Her raven hair was in two long French braids, pulled to the back, baby hairs laying down on her oatmeal colored forehead and temples. Even during the winter months, Penelope's Brazilian tan went nowhere.

"Big Body came through checking for you. Said get with him. It's important. That nigga Ross and Meek having a party tonight too," Sacari said.

"We going," Mes'siyah returned, wondering what Big Body was up to, and watching Penelope approach at the same time.

"Say that," Sacari shot back.

"Be through around eleven. Peace."

Penelope stood with her legs crossed and glowing, lips real glossy. She was happy Mes'siyah had sent for her. In her eyes, he was her man. In her head, the King mansion was her home. *And*, she was getting paid to do something she loved doing.

"So, what's up?" she said, then poked out her bottom lip, which was juicy by nature. Just like her thighs, her tits, and her behind.

"What I tell you about being in my room?"

"Not to." She backed up a little as he got closer.

"So why were you in my room, touching my bed?"

"I wasn't in your room, Mes'siyah."

Mes'siyah grabbed her by her jaw, as he stepped closer. He always knew when she was lying. He inhaled her fragrance which as coming from her cleavage, and said, "Find out who was." After he said that, he let his tongue drag slightly up her throat. She closed her eyes, biting her bottom lip as he said, "You hear me, Penelope?"

"I do." She was startled as his hand slid up her skirt, maneuvering her lace panties to the side. "And I will, bae," she promised as his fingers slipped inside her vagina. "Ahhh, that feels so good, Mes'siyah."

"I'ma stuff this dick down your throat til you can't breathe, if you don't find out," he threatened as his thumb rotated on her protruding clit. "Understand me?"

"I do, lover…"

Angel's voice came through the intercom, "Son, where are you?"

Penelope adored Mes'siyah, especially when he spoke to her filthy. The more explicit, the more she was turned on. Made her feel desired by him, and necessary.

Mes'siyah took his fingers from her, slipped them in

her lips and tongue, then his hungry mouth enjoyed the rest of her wetness. "You taste as good today as you did the first time I tasted that nectar, you sexy Bee," he whispered pass the diamond stud in her right earlobe.

"I wanna taste you," she whispered back. "It's been a while, and I want that dick in my mouth, my pussy, my ass too, daddy."

"I know," he returned, before smacking her on her ass, sending her off. "Got a date with moms though."

"Maybe later?" she asked seductively. Each time they went at it seemed to top the last.

"Mes'siyah!" Angel called.

Penelope went one way, and he went the other. They really believed no one in the house knew what was going on between them. Angel had known since Mes'siyah was seventeen, but said nothing. Rubi accidently caught Mes'siyah fucking Penelope one night when their parents were in the South of France. And, the rest of the staff, *oh*, they just did their jobs and kept their mouths shut.

Angel was at the bottom of the swirling staircase in a crimson curve hugging one-piece dress, looking like she was twenty again. Her hair was in an upsweep do, her diamond choker was glistening, and her wedding ring could be noticed from miles away. She as ready to roll.

Mes'siyah opened the passenger side door for her, and they hopped in the G-Wagon. Inside, as she fastened her seatbelt, she said, "Sometimes it feels like you were just sixteen-years-old, standing three feet tall, if that. *Now*, you are taller than your dad, and driving me around...."

Mes'siyah chuckled and smiled as he fastened his seatbelt, knowing Angel wouldn't allow him to drive her anywhere without that seatbelt on. He looked over at her, wanting to say, *And running the city!*

"Ma, you so melodramatic..."

Mother and son talked and filled the luxury Mercedes with laughter, all the way to the fanciest restaurant in Villanova. Then Angel asked about the family she left behind in New York City, twenty-two years ago.

"I only saw Jamal," he said, looking over at her. He knew the backstory, Angel's humble beginnings before getting rich. His grandmother's horrible parenting and allegiance to the crack-pipe, and the father she never knew. "But, I told him to give auntie your number."

"One day I want to get us all together, even my mom, and just enjoy each other's company. You know?"

"Clearly."

"If I didn't meet your father, I don't know who I'd be today. He believed in me. He wanted my heart, not just my body. You know?"

That conversation carried on until they were seated. Mes'siyah was the only person she could vent to, have those heartfelt conversations with, and not be guarded.

"So, you know your father is bringing in new staff?"

"What you mean?"

"Two more cooks, and three new maids."

"I ain't with all that, ma. Them niggah coming in the house and all that."

"But, it's cool for them bitches to be prancing around

all up in *my* shit?"

"I can read bitches," he said, picking up the menu. "They gonna live with us, and want one thing…"

"And what is that?"

"What you think? Daddy don't be there long enough for them to want him."

"So, they want you?" asked Angel, smiling.

"Clearly," Mes'siyah said, peeking over the menu like he was a little kid being sneaky.

Honestly, Angel didn't know where Mes'siyah's swag came from. He possessed just the right blend of confidence and cockiness, from what she could see. He didn't cut corners, didn't sugarcoat things, and fought for what he believed in. Can't forget he was only 21. When Angel was his age, she was still making mistakes, when she and Bish were running con games on perverts down Center City. Every once in a while, they would fuck a package up, and owe the connect money, and together they would figure it out by pickpocketing, duping tricks, shit like that.

"Ma, can I order for us?"

Angel was snatched from her daydream. "Sure, son," she said, then got back to her cozy inner thoughts. She wondered why Mes'siyah wasn't in a serious relation-ship yet? Hadn't brought a woman home for the holidays yet? He was handsome, had finished high school, even got a few credits in college before deciding higher learning wasn't for him. *Or, even come out about Penelope???*

She thought this might be the time to tell him.

"I'm ordering chicken salads, with the works. Shrimp Alfredo, on the side."

"Mes'siyah, I want another baby..." Angel revealed. "I wanted a boy too. Before I'm forty. Me and ya dad been working on it."

Mes'siyah peeked over the menu again, then sat the menu down, running his hand over his flowing waves.

The waitress arrived, and Mes'siyah place the order. Within minutes, the appetizers arrived. Mes'siyah had a mozzarella stick, then said, "If you like it, I love it."

Angel wanted a baby she could raise outside of the life. A child she could send to one of those historical black colleges and universities. A *goodie two shoes* of some sort. Rubi ducked college, too busy being spoiled. And Mes'siyah was running things. Angel wanted one more shot at getting it right.

"You ain't bringing me a baby," Angel said, introducing a mozzarella stick to her mouth.

Like only he could, Mes'siyah said, "My *pull-out-game* is so tight! *Second to none.*"

"Ill, too much visual," she said, checking her iPhone.

"Ah, I thought that was you, Mrs. King," said a tall white man, his wife and daughter flanking him.

Angel looked up, slowly. "*Wow. Sydney Manning. Elvory Manning. And,* Ivory. What a surprise..."

District Attorney Manning was out having lunch with his family. He needed to get away from the office. He opened the two buttons on his sports blazer, and reached out to shake hands with Mes'siyah. *It was a firm shake.*

Mes'siyah looked from the white couple to their stunning daughter. Ivory looked from Mes'siyah to Angel, then back to Mes'siyah.

"Angel King," Elvory said, taking Angel's hand into her own. "You look as good today as you did at the last fundraiser."

"And you too," Angel replied, blushing.

Ivory simply said, "Hi," wondering how Mes'siyah's mother knew her and her mother. Her father, everyone knew. He was a public figure. A politician. On the news every other day.

"So, where's the big guy?" Manning asked. He was also thinking, *Mes'siyah is looking more like a gangster today than ever before.*

"Atlanta, on business, Sydney," Angel answered, noticing how intently Manning was staring at her son as they shook hands. "His private jet should be landing at Philadelphia International in the morning, where I'll be waiting. *God, I miss him.*"

"I bet you do. Alright, enjoy your lunch and your time together," Sydney Manning said, relinquishing Mes'siyah's hand. Then he strolled off with his wife and daughter.

Ivory stole one more look at Mes'siyah while he was playing *high post*, basically acting like he didn't notice her.

"Ma, she still looking?"

"She is," Angel told Mes'siyah.

Angel thought back to the day she and Bishop met Sydney Manning. Mes'siyah was in her belly, and Bish

48

was in a jail cell on State Road with no bail. Manning was at the Public Defender's Office, assigned to represent Bish. Manning had an affinity for black and brown women. Especially the young and nubile ones who could perform blow jobs. Angel was young and nubile, and willing to do anything to increase Bish's chances of being treated fairly in the criminal justice system.

Angel remembered, *Manning got the murder charge and conspiracy dropped at a Habeas Corpus Hearing, just six months into Bish's incarceration.*

"*...never forget the people who helped you along the way...*"

"What you say, ma?"

"Oh, nothing. Was just thinking to myself..."

BOOG DENIRO

CHAPTER FIVE

MAY 25, 2016
MONDAY 7:03 PM

It was 89 degrees in Philly. With the humidity, it felt like 106. The only good thing was, the temperature was dropping, and the sun would set soon. A cool breeze was coming through too. Mes'siyah and Sacari locked eyes for the third time in like two minutes, as they stood on 23rd and Berks. Mes'siyah scratched his head, and looked back to Tec, slightly confused.

"So you *don't* have my money?" Mes'siyah asked once again.

"Are you deaf?" Tec retorted.

Sacari flexed his muscles as he clenched his jaw, flaring his nostrils. Mes'siyah raised his eyebrows, forming wrinkles in her forehead.

"I said I'm not copping off you and ya pops. *Ya pops and you.* However the fuck y'all put it. Don't matter, ain't there no more. This ain't the Eighties, and y'all ain't the *black mafia,* or the *black hand.*"

"Clearly," Mes'siyah chuckled and pinched his nose, looking down at his red Dolce&Gabanna hightops.

"Period," Tec emphasized.

"So, what I'm trying to understand is, why you dancing around my question?"

"What was the question again?"

Mes'siyah said, "My money? You got it?" with even

more aggression in his voice.

"What the fuck is you talking about?" Tec said stepping closer with his stocky stature.

Sacari stepped up.

Mes'siyah outstretched his arm, stopping Sacari quickly. Sacari was going for his gun. Mes'siyah smirked, eyelids low and squinted, sun shining on his face. "Listen, business is business. You got my money or not?" Mes'siyah asked for the last time.

"You not out southwest. We don't give a fuck about you out here—"

Waock! Waock! Sacari hit him with a powerful uppercut and stiff jab. Tec fell on his back pockets, and everyone on the block that spring evening stood up.

"Chill, chill. We out," Mes'siyah said, opening the driver's side door to the Bentley.

"Hoe ass niggah." Sacari kicked Tec, just for good measure. It was always like Sacari was auditioning for the first time for the enforcer job. And it never got old. Mes'siyah loved it. *The fervor, and the loyalty.*

As Mes'siyah sped off, he called Bish.

"Young boy," Bish answered.

"Wussup, old head?"

"At the site for this new building we'll be renovating. Then, I have to stop by the studio, see where my money is going. And then, there's a meeting with the urban division of our clothing company. Why?"

"You got everybody info in the Bible, correct?"

"No question."

"Thanks. Have fun being a CEO...."

"Whispers is with me. You need him?"

"Got Sacari wit me," Mes'siyah said, changing lanes.

"Alright then," Bish said, then hung up.

Mes'siyah knew a couple of the dudes would try to rebel just to see if he could carry the load the way his father had for so long. Mes'siyah knew he was going to have to set the tone with some of these dudes. He also knew that Tec was one of the ones copping off those New York dudes. He had a private investigator tail Tec, and two other dudes his father had passed off to him. With Mally Gz doing so good, moving weight like crazy, Bish felt Mes'siyah was really ready. *But he wasn't*. Too emotional.

"We gotta tear down and rebuild the whole thing. Tell everybody be ready, and be ready for the location," he ordered, looking Sacari square in the eyes.

"Clearly," Sacari replied, pulling out his phone.

Mes'siyah dialed the PI's number. It was a white woman in her early forties. She said, "Mr. King?"

"Text me the location."

"Okay."

Two minutes later, the info came through. Mes'siyah pulled onto the Expressway treating the Bentley like a go-cart, zipping in and out of traffic.

"What up with Nico?"

Sacari said, "What up with him?"

"We gotta show him the *Royal way*. Take him under the wing."

"You think he ready?"

"He sixteen. He ready. I ain't saying throw him in

the lion's den, but make him our young boy. Turn his swagg up a bit," Mes'siyah said.

Sacari scratched his head.

"He watching us. Not too long ago he asked me to drop him off at school. He wanted to be seen in the Bentley. He want parts, bro."

Sacari scratched his head again. His moms worked a lot, was never home, but she was still strict and ran the household over the phone. The only reason Sacari was in the streets was because she couldn't control him. But Sacari thought Mes'siyah was right. Nico was always around, and he had been getting accused of being part of the gang already anyway.

While Sacari was thinking, Mes'siyah said, "I want him on the block too."

"Clearly," Sacari said, though he wasn't truly in agreement.

Mes'siyah pulled up to the gates of the King estate. The guards in the security booth had the gates opening when they peeped the Bentley coming. His tires squealed as he came around the oval pavement leading to the front of the house. He pulled the emergency brake. They both hopped out and trekked up the stairs and into the mansion. Mes'siyah shot straight to the Oval Office, while Sacari found Angel in the kitchen with some strangers.

Mes'siyah must've been studying the Bible for about thirty minutes when Bish entered with Whispers.

"Young Boy," Bish said, and Mes'siyah got up out the extraordinary chair that looked more like a thrown.

54

"Pops, unc…" Mes'siyah replied. "Back already?"

"Just wanted to see my wife for a second," Bish said.

"Youngin," Whispers said, in his low raspy vocals. He was looking at the book in Mes'siyah's hand that looked just like the King James version of the bible. It was really a ledger.

Bish's operation spanned from Philly to New York, from Camden to Virginia Beach, and even into Baltimore. *The prices allowed him such a span.*

Mes'siyah found names, numbers, addresses, and relations to Tec. He took a picture of the page, shut, the book, and slipped it back into the gigantic bookshelf behind his father's desk. Whispers wondered what was in it. It was the first time he'd ever seen it. And Bish peeped that.

As Mes'siyah was leaving out, Whispers said, "They gonna test you. Make sure you pass with flying colors."

"Clearly," Mes'siyah said with a smirk. He exited the office, and went straight to the kitchen where the new chefs and maids were. Angel was walking them through things for her upcoming dinner party, while Sacari watched her. Mes'siyah waved him over.

As they were leaving out, Rubi was coming in with her Chanel shades on, hair and Prada bag swinging.

"Brother," she said, flanked by three of her badass girlfriends. She picked up the 58th Street piece on Mes'siyah's chain and said, "So icy." She had a link around her neck too, covered in all VVS diamonds.

He pulled her to the side, said, "Did I make myself clear.? *Clearly or unclearly?*"

Rubi cocked her head to the side, looked Mes'siyah up and down. "I only have one father."

"Yeah, okay. Let me see you in Vanity, Onyx, or Da Zip again. And we'll see."

"Mes'siyah, I finished school. *I'm grown.*"

"Come here for a minute," he said, taking her by the arm. As soon as they got into the foyer, Mes'siyah grabbed Rubi by her throat, and pushed her against the wall. With his free hand, he took the designer shades off the bridge of her nose. *"Clearly or unclearly?"*

"You're hurting me," she squealed.

"Clearly or unclearly?"

"Clearly..." Rubi seethed through clenched teeth.

$ $ $

RUBI, 9:57 PM

"But mom..."

"Ah, ah, ahh," Angel cut her off, raising her hands defensively. "I don't want to hear it. Unless you're telling on yourself too. I know my son, and he ain't going to choke you for nothing. You must've did something."

"Daddy!" Rubi cried, storming out of the master bed.

"What the fuck I just said?" Angel snapped, moving at the same pace as Rubi, and catching up to her.

"OMG!" Rubi sulked, stopping in her tracks. She was Daddy's little girl. So yeah she shed a few fake tears to get her brother checked like a pair of Nikes.

He had embarrassed her, and violated her personal space. She had to do something, and she wanted the same liberties he had. *Free to do as she pleased.*

Bish was coming their way in his smoker's jacket, pajama pants and house shoes. "Did I hear you call me, Rubi King?"

Rubi looked back at her mother. Yes, she was the princess, but Angel was the *muthafuckin'* Queen. "Yea, I just wanted to say goodnight, and thanks for everything you do for me, and *my brother...*"

Bish kissed Rubi on the forehead, said, "Your neck looks a little red. What's up with that???"

"It's nothing. Was playing around with the girls in the pool a little while ago," Rubi lied.

Bish said, "Okay, goodnight. Talk to you."

Rubi made her way around to the other side of the mansion. She was vexed, and in total disbelief. *Bish was supposed to be her protector, not just her provider, right? There was supposed to be no favorites, right?* Well, not that night.

As soon as Rubi got to her room, her girlfriend said, "Did it work?"

Rubi was embarrassed to tell her what really transpired, so she said, "I'm Daddy's little princess..." Then, she took off her robe. Underneath was a salacious purple crop-top and a distressed mini that hugged Rubi's curves too much.

"I think you should've just left it alone," girlie said.

Rubi sat at her vanity, and just stared at her friend through the mirror. She wiped the blush from her neck, which was there because she knew her father would notice it, and identify it as a bruise. As she did her makeup, her friend said, "They treat Mes'siyah like he's a god."

"Key word...*like*. He's not a god," Rubi shot back as she applied lip liner to her succulent lips, then applied the Juicy Couture lip gloss for flare. Her lips now looked full and seductive. She added pink blush to her high yellow cheeks, then put on her gold choker embedded with rubies and diamonds. And then some dangling diamond earrings. After that, the baby hair got laid down, and her tresses were pulled back and low into a neat ponytail.

After checking her angels in the mirror, and approving, she said, "Almost done."

"Bitch, if you don't hurry up!"

"Shut up, Imani," Rubi shot back, lining her perfectly arched brows. Then the eyeliner made her bright hazel eyes pop. She blinked and checked her angles once again. "And roll the weed up, bitch," Rubi ordered.

Last, Rubi put on some eye shadow. She didn't even need makeup, but it made her look a little more *vixenish*. And a bit more mature.

Now came the shoes. There were so many to choose from. The same with her purses and handbags. If Mes'siyah was treated like a god, Rubi got the goddess treatment. They were truly *urban royalty*.

With her reflection in a full body mirror staring back at her, Rubi said, "*There we go...*" Her 5'2" bowlegged frame was going to make the fellas go crazy.

Rubi had a tiny waist, shapely hips, athletic thighs, a pretty ass, and cute C-cups. She was going on nineteen, but looked much older. The Instagram models sometimes trolled her because she had naturally what they paid to have enhanced.

Imani was nice too. Thick as some fresh fudge, shaped right, half Black half Rican. But she would trade all that for the bejeweled Christian Louboutin's Rubi had chosen to sport. *Fuck the Rolex on Rubi's wrist!* Imani wanted the shoes.

To take her mind off the envy, Imani lit up the fat blunt of OG Kush that she had just rolled.

"What the fuck???" Rubi snapped. "This is a ten million dollar house...you gonna stain walls. Mes'siyah don't even smoke in the house. *Fuck wrong with you?*"

Imani put the weed out, and they were gone. On their way to UNCUT.

$ $ $

"Nah, leave the logo next to him," Mes'siyah urged, putting the four duffel bags over his shoulder, two on either shoulder, walking out of Tec's crib. The gang followed closely behind, pulling off their gloves. Mes'siyah put the bags in the trunk of the 550 Benz.

"Where lil Bro?" Sacari asked.

Down their calling *earl*," replied Mes'siyah.

Nico was bent over, vomit bursting from his mouth in some lady's rose garden. They hopped in the cars, and Sacari slowly pulled alongside of his baby bro.

"Young boy," Sacari said, as the tinted window slowly came down. "You alright?"

"Waaa?" Nico used the back of his hand to wipe his mouth, then out came, "Why his brains look like that?"

Sacari and Mes'siyah both laughed at him, recalling their first kill.

"Get ya lil' as in the car," Sacari ordered, while looking up and down the dark suburban street.

Nico followed orders, then was tossed a bottle of water to rinse his mouth. The '09 Benz peeled off with water from Nico's mouth flying through the air. Mes'siyah then handed Nico a tightly rolled Backwood for him to spark up.

"Don't sweat it, you'll get used to it, eventually," he told Nico.

"That's what y'all do, huh?" Nico said, sucking smoke into his young lungs.

Mes'siyah smirked, turning forward, and Sacari glanced back at Nico.

"When our hand is forced," Sacari replied. He never wanted this for his brother. *But, Mes'siyah always got what Mes'siyah wanted.*

Sacari turned the music up, and apparent became Drake's voice. His latest hit *Summer Sixteen!*

As if nothing had happened that night, the gang pulled up at Boston Market and piled in there six deep. They were loud, laughing, joking, bragging, and boasting about everything from new music videos, to the 76ers playoff push, to chicks. But the work they had put in never came up.

Then Mes'siyah's phone rang. Things got quiet. It was Big Body. He wanted some powder, and to let Me'siyah know that the linebacker had been back that next day inquiring about him. That made him think about Ivory...

Not even a minute later, she was calling him. With one foot on the floor, and the other outstretched across the booth seat, he said, "What up?"

"Just checking on you," she said, then added, "I did some homework on you."

"Oh yeah?" Mes'siyah looked at his *bust down* Rolex, stirring the straw in his drink. "Anything good?"

Before she could answer, he hung up, and called her on FaceTime. She answered.

"Anyhow, just wanted you to know I wanted you to call me, whenever you have time. The only reason I hadn't reached out sooner is because... I thought your mom was one of your hoochie fans."

Mes'siyah laughed. Angel definitely didn't look like she was pushing forty, and she had never been under the knife. Her exquisite beauty was natural, but he resembled her so much that anyone could see he came from her. That's why he laughed.

Ivory said, "I wanted to be sitting with you, so I didn't see the striking resemblance. I only saw an attractive woman who looked really happy to be in your presence." Now blushing, she took her intense gaze from Mes'siyah.

"A brother had you jealous?"

"I like you."

Licking his lips, Mes'siyah said, "I fucks with you too."

"Ivory, who is that? Got you all giddy and giggling and blushing and whatnot?" That was Ivory's girlfriend getting all in the screen. She was shocked when she saw Mes'siyah's face staring back at her.

He said, "Clearly…" then chucked the deuces.

"Her lil' white ass done fell for a gangster," her girlfriend added, making room for the rest of their girl gang to get in the screen.

Mes'siyah chucked the deuces again as his gang got into the screen too. Even with all the commotion all around them, Mes'siyah and Ivory's eyes never lost contact. Everything Mes'siyah wanted was falling right into his lap. More money, more clientele, and a chick he thought he could finally take serious.

CHAPTER SIX

JUNE 3, 2016
MONDAY, 3:03 PM

Now, the streets was talking. The death of Tec, with the logo of the Bull spray painted on the wall sent a stark message. A raging bull was stamped on each and every kilo that Bish bought from the Mexican Cartel down in El Paso, Texas. Everyone who copped off Bish knew this. Which was why Bish was shaking his head when he found out Mes'siyah had pulled that move. But, it was the young boy's show, and Bish was going to let him run it—*win, lose or draw*.

Besides all the talk about who put Tec down and why, Big Body was moving the blow at a fast pace right on the premises of Ocean Palms.

Mes'siyah was sitting in the Bentley with a fistful of golden tresses in his grasp. The chick's head was going up and down, up and down, in his lap, and traces of her saliva was all over his manhood.

She looked up and said, "What does *clearly* mean?"

"It a statement, an energizer, a motivator. It's not what you're saying, it's how you're saying it..." he replied, burying her face back in his lap so she could get back to sucking the eight and a half inches of hard flesh.

He was parked right in the parking lot of Ocean Palms, in the midst of a sea of luxury cars, being sucked feverishly when his phone sounded off and Ivory's face appeared on his screen.

Mes'siyah didn't hesitate to answer. "Ivory, what's good?" he asked with his left arm resting on the door panel so she could only see his body from the chest up.

A minute into the call, he was explaining the definition of *clearly* again. This time to Ivory. "It can mean: *yes*; *no*; *you know better*; or it can mean what it says—*clearly*," he said, clearly trying to conceal what was going on in the car.

Ivory said, "Whatever..." And then, "I think it's really cute though. I catch myself saying it now."

You're looking cute, with those big books laid out all over that huge canopy bed. And, in those pink boy shorts, tight white Tee, with tha feet all out, thought Mes'siyah as he continued to get head.

"Studying, huh?" Mes'siyah liked that, because the chicks he was banging and getting deep throated by weren't into book. Most were into the streets. So seeing Ivory like that turned him on something crazy.

"I am. A thesis on criminal justice reform in the great state of Pennsylvania, for my professor. There's a great need for it."

"Well, you better get back to work. Hit me up when you finish..." he said, his breathing a bit labored now.

Ivory thought she saw blonde locks in Mes'siyah's grips, but kept it to herself because she wasn't sure. And he had pretty much ended the call abruptly.

Thaila flung her hair to the side and looked up at Mes'siyah before going back to work. Her moans became increasingly louder as Mes'siyah pumped into her warm and moist mouth. She was in her late twenties but sucked meat like she'd been doing it forever. So clearly, Mes'siyah was enjoying it. In her white cat-suit by Philly designer Ms. Cat, Thaila slid deeper into his lap, licking, sucking, kissing and yanking his dick.

Nico walked up to the window, the slurps and gags becoming deeper, and Mes'siyah let the window down. Nico said, "What up, Big Bro? Can I get some of that?"

"That ain't why you're here. I'll get ya dick sucked later. Plus, broads I do don't do groups." Mes'siyah let that settle in, then said, "I need you to grab that, and get it to Big Body. That's what you here for. You dig?"

"Clearly..." Nico replied.

"Yo," Mes'siyah said, stopping him.

Nico about-faced, braids swinging, and said, "Yeah."

"Stop acting like you ain't seen a dick suck, when you've seen a dick suck. You with me, we them boys."

Nico said, "Ya bitches be the baddest."

"I feel you. And you better believe it. You next."

"Clearly..."

Mes'siayh leaned back, brought the tint back up. Then an urge came to mind. From his impulsive side. *The unnecessary shit.* He Face-timed Ivory, and when she appeared on the screen he didn't say anything, just tapped the screen initiating the backside camera, showing him palming Thaila's head as it went up and down. "*Clearly...*" He tapped the screen, using the frontal camera while his dick disappeared in the woman's mouth.

"What the fuck???" Ivory howled. She was livid. "I

know this dude didn't—"

"Ivory, once we start fucking, all this will come to an end," he said, licking his lips.

Ivory quickly hung up. Immediately, he wondered had he overplayed his hand. Thaila just giggled, and got back to trying to make Mes'siyah erupt.

He pushed himself as far down her throat as he could, a few good times, and globs and streams of fluids shot down the woman's throat. She sucked and sucked until every drop was hers. Barely able to breath, she managed to give him a warm smile so that he knew she was enjoying pleasuring him.

"You good?" he asked afterwards and awkwardly.

She nodded seductively, retrieving a baby wipe from her purse. After opening the door, spitting on the asphalt, cleaning her and Mes'siyah up, she said, "I have to find your dad a house in the hills of Calabasas. And it is not easy."

"Calabasas, as in … *Kardashian land*???"

Thaila was Bish's Realtor, half Black, half Asian, and secretly crushed on Bish for years. But Bish was loyal to Angel, so she got with his son. She spat in the street again. "They didn't tell you, they're moving?"

"Nah." There was a pause, and then, "Alright, I'll be through later on tonight to handle that for you."

"Good because my husband hasn't fucked him in a month. I need some dee."

Mes'siyah zipped his jeans up, didn't say much. He was selfish. Even though Thaila was married, and had a life of her own, he didn't like hearing about her home

"What you just did to that woman wasn't nice, Mr. King," Thaila said, jokingly and though she didn't mind. Wasn't like her face could be seen.

"I'll make it up to her."

"Are you ever going to settle down?"

"I'm thinking about it."

"Why haven't you busted that open yet?"

"Good girl."

"I was a good girl, didn't stop you from busting this open," Thaila said.

"I ain't choose you, you chose me," Mes'siyah said.

LATER THAT NIGHT, Mes'siyah fucked the real estate maven's brains out, made her orgasm multiple times, then went to the block and hung out with the gang.

Ms. Gloria was on the scene. She was the *neighborhood mom*, feeding, clothing and mentoring a number of the at-risk youth. She even did outreach to the teen moms going through pregnancy for the first time. She had the hustler's utmost respect, and especially Mes'siyah's. So when she asked him to do something for the kids, he would get his philanthropy on.

Following that conversation, Mes'siyah located Nico. He ruffled his plaits while saying, "How much did Big Body give you?"

"I'll be right back."

"Wait, wait. You didn't count it?"

"That's ya folks. I didn't think I had to."

"Something like that could fall on you. If it's short,

even though he my folks. Tighten up."

"It won't happen again. If my brother give me something for you, I'm counting it."

"Clearly!"

Nico didn't like being checked, and chastised, especially in front of the gang. It was dark out, but the lights on the porch made it possible for him to lock eyes with Sacari before taking off. In minutes, Nico returned with a super thick was of cash. He said, "Fifteen racks."

"Take one for yourself." Mes'siyah said.

As Nico was peeling off $1,000, Mes'siyah walked down the block a little with Cash. Cars were passing by, hitting the horns, giving Mes'siyah shout outs. But his attention belonged to Cash. Facing Cobbs Creek Parkway, Cash said, "*Smally G* ring a bell?"

"You mean my cousin, Mally Gz? Yeah, that's my heart. He in the Bronx doing his numbers..."

"I said, *Smally G*?" Cash reiterated. "I know who Mally Gz is. Remind me of dem COKE BOYS niggas."

Smally G was Bish's right-hand man. The two had embarked upon the street life together, right out the sandbox, eventually making trips to N.Y. on re-ups. That's also where Smally G met Angel when she was just an around-the-way girl, roaming the Bronx streets aimlessly. Or so Smally G thought. Angel was a visionary at seventeen, and could see that Bish was the true don of their little outfit. And since she had never loved Smally G anyway, it was rather easy to fall for Bish's charming ass when he came at her behind Smally's G's back.

While Bish was secretly romancing Angel, the two crime partners were arrested on Murder One charges together. Some dude had violated them when he robbed Smally G, stripping him naked in front of millions, on West Market Street, that hot summer evening in 1996. So, he had to go. Somehow, Sydney Manning managed to get Bish off, while tons of evidence against Smally G led to him pleading out. Smally G received 19 to 40 years, while Bish went on to erect a massive empire *that even Cookie and Lucious had to salute.*

Mes'siyah didn't know Smally G personally. But he'd heard the stories, even seen pictures of the OG on several social media outlets. "Cash, get to it!" he ordered like a boss.

"Word is, he just made parole."

Me'siyah scratched his bearded cheek, watching cars travel the street. He wondered if his father knew about this, and whether or not this had anything to do with Bish's sudden desire to move out of Philly, and make Mes'siyah the new *King of the town*???

Cash was running his hand over his thick wavy hair.

Mes'siyah looked him up and down, said, "What?"

"...da niggah Stones?"

Stones was grabbing bricks off Bish. He was a long hair perm wearing Pimp style cat. He's been in it to win it since the nineties, moving bass with Bish at an alarming rate. He had the streetwalkers, the hoes, and the trannies doing numbers for him.

"What about him?" asked Mes'siyah.

"That's my cousin's baby's father's uncle," Cash relayed, making Mes'siyah mad. He hated when Cash started the gossiping shit, when it wasn't advantageous.

"Okay? What's up?"

"Long story short, Stones ain't feeling copping off a dude twenty-five years younger than him."

"Oh yeah?"

"He grabbing off some N.Y. dudes now. They got the Coca Cola logo on their bricks. My cousin getting that shit dropped on her ass now. And, Stones running his mouth like a bitch..."

Mes'siyah's face glowed under the light of the street lamp. Cash saw his thick eyebrows tighten. His freakishly long lashes could not shield the fire in Mes'siyah's brown eyes either. Again, he caressed his beard while licking his lips before brushing his thumb over the birthmark on his right cheek. "*I like resistance.*"

"There's more," Cash told Mes'siyah.

"More???" Mes'siyah couldn't use anymore. He was still reeling about that disgusting thing he's done to Ivory Manning. He frowned, folding his tattooed arms over his frail chest. "Go ahead..."

"It's this dude out Kensington on Ruth and Orleans run like four or five blocks, caseworker, driving a cherry red bombed out Q45 coupe."

"What about him?"

"He's fucking Rubi. And, she not his main squeeze."

The hairs on Mes'siyah's arms and neck rose, and at the very same time his nostrils flared.

"They call him Trap God," Cash exposed.

Mes'siyah was furious. "God? I'm the Mes'siyah!"

"Huh?" Cash said, bewildered that Mes'siyah was making this about him.

"Me! I'm the chosen one! And you're telling me he's jacking my swagg!!!"

"And, smashing Rubi..."

It wasn't long before Mes'siyah and the gang was turning down Ruth and Orleans. The 550 was leading the way with the Range Rover tailing the Bentley.

Pointing, Sacari said, "There go her girlfriend's Honda Accord right there Bro."

Mes'siyah couldn't front, Kensington was looking like something out of *New Jack City*! Fiends were scattered about, moving frantically in hunt of crack rock and herion.

"And there is Rubi's Porsche truck," Sacari added.

Mes'siyah slowed up, stopping next to the Porsche. He pulled the emergency brake, then grabbed his twin shoulder holsters out the back seat. He opened the door, and all of the doors opened. He exited the Bentley, and ran down on the Porsche. He cupped his hands, looking through the tint. No one was inside.

"Rubi, ain't that your bro?" Mes'siyah heard, and turned in that direction.

"What? Word? Where?" he heard Rubi say as he stalked around the Porsche and seen a burning Backwood in Rubi's hand, smoke pluming from her lips and nostrils. Her legs were dangling over some dudes thighs as he attempted to suck the smoke exiting her mouth into his. Her girls and a few of his boys were boo'd up as well.

The dude doing the shotgun with Rubi was wearing a big gold chain with a medallion reading TRAP GOD. Rubi's ass cheek was in one of his hands, and the other hand held a bottle of Rose.

"Oh shit," Rubi chimed, attempting to put some space between her and the Trap God.

Mes'siyah grabbed her by her hair, and she had that good stuff. *All done up too!* He damn near dragged Rubi off the steps. A burly fellow in Nike joggers and a tight Tee tried to play hero. *"That's a woman—"*

Mes'siyah moved so quick, pulling his gold 50cal Dessert Eagle, placing it to dude's left clavicle. *BOOM!* The dude's body snapped back, and Rubi screamed. Trap God jumped, dropping the bottle, breaking it, as his man's body slid clean across the pavement. Sacari and Nico, along with the rest of the gang, had their triggers trained. People were running, screaming, even covering their eyes...to see no evil.

Mes'siyah yanked Rubi by her hair, as his nostrils flared, gripping his pistol tightly at the same time.

"Wait, wait, wait..." Rubi urged. "My stuff, 'siyah."

He looked back, seen her Gucci bag, but still shoved her into the Bentley. "My car!" she was shouting, arms and legs flailing. Once in the back seat, Mes'siyah slammed the door on her hard as shit.

In the distance police sirens could be heard. Someone had called in the shooting. The shock in Mes'siyah's gang's eyes could not be missed. They all headed to the cars while Sacari grabbed Rubi's bad and pulled off him her Porsche.

"If I hear about you even looking at my sister again, that will be the last bitch you ever look at," Mes'siyah forewarned then rolled out.

Inside the Bentley, Rubi told Mes'siyah, "I wasn't doing anything! Why you tripping?"

"Shut the fuck up," Mes'siyah said, yanking the steering wheel left, racing up a ramp, evading the sirens.

Weaving in and out of traffic, Mes'siyah found his way to the front of the pack his gang was leading.

"Why would you do that?" Rubi quizzed, leaning in over the console.

Mes'siyah ignored her. She would never understand. The king name was sacred to him, and meant something in the streets and the industry. He couldn't have dudes preying on his little sister. He couldn't have her watering down the brand. At that moment, a call came in from Bish. He answered, and through the speakers, Bish said, "Young boy..."

"Where you at, old head?" he asked his father, and Bish immediately took notice to the uneasy temperament.

"At the palace. Why, what's up?"

"We got a problem, and we need to rap."

Rubi sighed, rolled her eyes, before sucking her teeth. She was certain Mes'siyah was going to rat her out. And would leave out the fact that he shot someone in front of mad people.

Bish said, "I need to see you when you get here."

For most of the ride to the King compound, it was quiet. Until Rubi said, "I wasn't even doing anything."

"Shut the fuck up. And, if I catch you with that bitch Imani again—"

"Wait, Imani is good peoples. She's actually doing something with herself. Like, getting her degree."

Mes'siyah turned around so quickly, left hand gripping the steering wheel, with fire in his eyes. He cocked his right hand back and slapped Rubi.

Rubi had real good reflexes, so the true impact of his anger wasn't felt. "Fuck you, Mes'siyah…"

Had he not been racing down the expressway, his aim would've been more accurate. With his elbow planted against the driver seat, propelling him forward, Mes'siyah zigzagged through lanes, with his gang tailing. Rubi watched him in shock.

Mes'siyah had been in 32 high speed chases and never got caught, or crashed out. He wasn't worried about the cops, he was worried about how he was going to hold this family together with all the unforeseen distractions looming.

Rubi looked back and saw Sacari driving her car like it was a *hooptie* or a *squatter*. She was pissed.

When they finally got through the front gates of the mansion, the gang veered off in the other direction. Sacari abandoned the Porsche and caught a cab.

"Look at my car!" Rubi shouted, as she examined the Porsche truck. Her flaps were muddy, the spoiler had scrapes, but more than anything, her personal space felt violated. *He left a spent Newport in my ashtray!!!*

Mes'siyah went straight to the office and sat on the throne. Bish was nowhere to be found, so he texted his father.

Bish opened the secret passage maybe a minute later, stating, "I'm never later..."

"Three things..."

"Clearly," Bish said, mocking his son, and sitting on the edge of his desk.

"I need complete control. I need you to trust and believe in me. I can't keep running back here, requesting permission. Just green lights, pop. I need you to know I can handle making big decisions, not just small ones."

Bish checked his fresh manicure and cuticles, then the fat rocks in his wedding ring, before scratching him salt-n-pepper waves with all ten fingers. Then he rubbed his bright hazel eyes, before looking at his son again. "Three strikes..."

"I'm the king?"

"I will always be the king of this family, Mes'siyah."

Mes'siyah smiled, said, "Clearly..."

"The other two things?" Bish asked.

"You and mommy want a third child?"

Bish's forehead wrinkled.

Mes'siyah said, "She told me a couple weeks ago. And I just want you to know, I know about the move to Cali too."

"Big facts, son. I met you mother in the Bronx twenty something years ago, and I've been happy since. We got fly together, we got high together, and I hope we die together."

Mes'siyah nodded, then asked, "Smally G; what's up

with that niggah, pops?"

"Old player. Loud, flashy, good looking, smart, and...if I'm not mistaken, he's up at Fayette State Prison."

"He's coming home in a couple weeks," Mes'siyah said, looking into his father's eyes.

Bish inhaled his next breath a little harder than the last, then stretched while cracking his neck. "Damn, it's been twenty years already?"

"Did you know?"

"I got arrested with him. I was with him when he laid the murder game down. But, I was blessed. Yeah, I had an idea..."

"Is that why you got Thaila looking for a home out in Calabasas for you and mommy?"

"Young boy, don't you ever disrespect my gangster like that again. You heard?"

"Clearly," Mes'siyah said, submissively. Bish was the only man on earth he would ever back down to. But he still had his suspicions, which put Smally G on Mes'siyah's radar.

After leaving Mes'siyah in the office, Bish went upstairs to the master bed, where the gorgeous Angel was waiting for him...*ass hole naked*. She was dead serious about conceiving her third child, and had been fucking Bish silly lately. "Everything okay?" she asked, crawling across their California king bed, reaching for his belt buckle.

"Smally G made parole."

She undressed Bish, then ran her right foot with the

bright white toenails over his flaccid manhood. It got hard instantly.

Bish grabbed her by her ankles, pulling her to the edge of the bed. He kissed her toes, said, "I wouldn't know you if it wasn't for him..."

"And I wouldn't know the woman I am today, if it wasn't for you," Angel shot back as her big toe of her left foot slipped into Bish's mouth.

"I think we should cut the talk then, and put on some JODECI..."

"I like the way you think, handsome..."

CHAPTER SEVEN

JUNE 4, 2016
TUESDAY 4:30 AM

The right hand man of the Trap God knew the code. *It was so street.* When detectives came to his hospital bedside showing him a lineup with Mes'siyah in it, he told them, "I didn't see him."

And, even after Mes'siyah warned Trap God about fucking with his little sister, Trap God had fallen to sleep while Face-timing Rubi.

On the other hand, Mes'siyah was sparking a Newport 100, as he crossed his legs on Stones' nightstand. Smoke escaped his nostrils as he leaned in his two-piece Dickies set. He nodded his head, and Nico punched Stones in the eye dumb hard, waking him from his peaceful slumber. A 12-gauge being held by Sacari was pointed at the other eye. But, all Stones could see was the cherry of the Newport, as Mes'siyah took another massive pull.

"What...the...fuck?" Stones said, when the brightness of Mes'siyah's flashlight shined in his face.

Sacari kicked Stones in the head and said, "Shut ya bitch ass up!"

Muffles could be heard coming from the foot of the bed, causing Stones to lean forward. He saw his young child and main squeeze bound and gagged.

Mes'siyah turned the flashlight off, asking, "Do you

know who I am?"

Stones squinted, but the vision in his right eye was impaired. Stones was in great shape for his age, but he knew he was outmatched, so he chose his words wisely. "I'm sorry, but I don't. Please introduce yourself?" he said.

"The new king of the town," Mes'siyah warned, taking another hard pull.

Stones immediately knew he was dealing with young boys, and tried to lunge forward with his hands outstretched. He was hoping to latch onto Mes'siyah's skinny neck, but Sacari spazzed. *WHACK! WHACK! WHACK!* Blood gushed from Stones' face as he fell to the floor at Mes'siyah feet.

Mes'siyah pulled a brick of coke from the duffel, tossing the kilo on the plastic covered floor, by Stones, logo upright for his viewing pleasure.

Stones said, "Bish's kid, huh?"

"Yeah," Mes'siyah said, lungs full of smoke. Then he said, "The bitch, Jack-Jack!"

Jack-Jack was moving on pure adrenaline, returning Stones' 17-year old daughter to her father's huge bedroom.

"Line 'em up at the foot of the bed," Mes'siyah ordered.

Cash pulled the 5-year old, throwing her in the mix next to her mother, who was next to the 17-year old.

Stones tried to buck back, but Sacari beat him until the back of his head opened up. Stones refused to lose consciousness though.

"I want to know where you got this brick from?" Mes'siyah asked, having located Stones' stash while he rested. It had the *Coca Cola* stamp on it.

When Stones didn't reply, Nico said, "Is this where I come in at, old head?" He was moving in on the 17-year old daughter, whom was in just a T-shirt and bikini cut panties.

Mes'siyah said, "That's right. I did tell you I was going to get your dick sucked, didn't I?"

Deep down, Mes'siyah was praying it didn't come down to that. That level of ruthlessness just didn't exist in him. *At least, not yet.* And, he most certainly believed in karma. Which is why he was so hard on Rubi. *Gangsters will do anything to make their point.*

As Nico moved closer to the nubile offspring of Stones, squeezing his dick to make it nice and hard, Mes'siyah said, "Wait. I wanna ask this fool one thing."

Nico was about to rip the duct tape from the daughter's mouth, and prepared to make Stones watch him make love to her mouth.

"What you got against working with a young nigga?" Mes'siyah asked Stones.

Stones was no fool. He said, "Nothing." And to get this over with sooner than later, he went on to add, "Check the papi store on the corner of 27th and Croosky. There's your competition." He barely had enough energy to talk, but he had got out just enough words before losing consciousness.

"Now, where's the money?"

Stones was clearly unable to respond.

Mes'siyah ripped the duct tape from him lady's mouth. She told Mes'siyah, "The old Acura Legend out back. Check the trunk."

Nico went to the gold Legend coupe, popped the trunk. In the space where a spare tire would normally be was a handmade leather satchel, the same shape and size of an 18" wheel. The sun was coming up, but they were in a very low key area of Northeast. Nico fingered the countless stacks, then sent Mes'siyah a text...GOT IT.

That's when Mes'siyah turned the lights on. Stones' lady saw the body bags. Then she saw that the dry wall was off the wall, exposing wires, beams and open space. Then the nail gun and tarp. *She was certain it was Bish's son.* She also knew they were about to be bodied, bodies never to be found.

And that's exactly what happened.

They moved in sync, stuffing the bodies in the bags, the bags into the walls, before nailing them to the pillars, then sealing the wall shut.

With everything put back in place, they vanished through the back roads.

BY NOON, MES'SIYAH was walking into the papi store on 27th and Croosky.

Sacari told the others, "Shoot anybody who come out. Three to the head. Make sure they down for the count."

Nico looked up the block, then down the block as he watched his big brother follow their leader. He wanted to be walking in there, not waiting outside. He pulled a

81

pack of Newports from his pocket, then a lighter, and sparked up. As soon as he took a puff, the door burst open and screaming and gunfire could be heard.

Nico snatched up his shirt and pulled his gat. At first he fumbled. And then: *Bocka! Bocka! Ba-ba-ba-ba-ba!* Nico shot any and everything moving. He picked up the cigarette that had fallen from his mouth, then tracked the woman crawling towards safety. *Three to the head.*

Newport hanging from his lips, he tracked the other dude down too. More shots were heard, and smoke was escaping Nico's gun.

Whistling an unfamiliar tune, Mes'siyah emerged twirling a surveillance disk on his index finger.

They got into the cars and pulled off. Sacari didn't feel right knowing his baby brother had begun dancing that thin line between sanity and insanity. And with those *fucking* braids dangling from his head, Nico was beginning to resemble O Dog from *Menace 2 Society*.

CHAPTER EIGHT

JUNE 19, 2016
WEDNESDAY, 2PM

On this particular day, Bish was in the office alone, going through the ledgers. He noticed the numbers were up in the streets, which made sense with dudes just disappearing, and new players filling their spots. But, Stones and his family going missing was weighing heavy on Bish. Almost as much as the shootings on 27th and Croosky. Someone close to Bish told him, *the cops knew a tall lanky dude was seen setting ablaze the getaway cars.*

Bish went back to the page where Mes'siyah crossed out Stones' name. Then he noticed Tec's name X'd out too. He wondered who would be voted off the island next???

"Bishop!" he heard. When he looked up, Angel was coming his way. She had come through the secret door, wearing stilettoes ... *and nothing else.* Her hair was in an upsweep do, and everything else was sitting up too. *Her tits, her ass, even her calves.*

Bish shut what looked like the King James version of the bible, logged out of the Mac Pro laptop he was tracking his legitimate business dealings on, and opened his zipper.

Upstairs, their son was glad his father wasn't asking a million and one questions about the *new King order.*

83

That made him feel real grown, real bossy. But at the same time, he knew Whispers was still lurking in the shadows.

With that out of his mind, he set out to find out why the scent of perfume was in his room. He hit the intercom...

"Penelope! Penelope!"

Moments later, "Yes...."

Mes'siyah said, "I need a minute."

While waiting, he leaned up against the seven-foot tall dresser, crossed his legs and arms, eyeing his bed sheets.

"You rang," Penelope said, cheesing, as she entered his bedroom.

"Did you find out who was in my room, like I told you?"

"Maybe..." she said, staring into his half-mast eyes.

"You ever seen me sleep on anything other than silk?"

"Nope."

"So who put the white *cotton* sheets on my bed?"

"I might leave something in here to let you know when I'm feinding for some sex, but I don't change sheets. It's the new girl," Penelope told him. "Joy is her name."

Without Mes'siyah even telling her to, Penelope left and returned with Joy. That's how well she knew him.

Joy reminded him of Amber Rose. Only, she had a head full of blonde hair instead of a low blonde cut. He told Penelope, "Go get the rest of the staff too."

Penelope did. And when they were all presents, Mes'siayh said to Joy, "I hear you may've changed my sheets?"

"I did," she said, smiling.

"Pack your things," Mes'siyah told her.

"Why?" she asked curiously.

Everyone but her knew what was coming next: "*You're fired.*"

"But I was only doing my job," Joy replied, while Penelope stood to the side smiling devilishly.

Mes'siyah paid Joy no mind. He looked to the others, male and female, and said, "You come in here, you're fired too. Back to work."

Penelope looked at him, and he lifted his brows. She kissed his cheek and left too, glad she would not have to compete with Joy for Mes'siyah's affection.

Just as he was laying across his bed to get some needed rest, Bish and Angel were finishing up their midday quickie with a dual shower, and preparing for a lunch date. Just the two of them. No security detail.

Joy was leaving out at the same time they were, and said, "Mrs. King, I love working here. It's my dream job to work for you guys. And your family."

"Okay," Angel said, filling her out yellow crystal-embellished silk jersey top and skirt by Moschino perfectly.

"Mes'siyah just fired me."

Angel and Bish looked at each other.

"Because I went in his room and changed his sheets," Joy shared with the power couple.

Bish said, "I know you weren't here long, but if you need a referral, have your next employer call me."

Joy was pissed.

As they were preparing to leave the compound, Bish told Angel, "Your son is really running things now."

"And, firing people I just hired…" Angel said, shaking her head. "I liked Joy too…" she added.

"The money on the streets is on the rise again, too," Bish said, strapping himself into his seatbelt and preparing to peel off in his black Phantom. Although they didn't want security, just wanted to be alone, that wasn't happening. A car pulled out behind them.

While they talked about Mes'siyah, he was dreaming. In the dream, he was chasing Ivory as she evaded him in four inch pumps, a crimson cap and gown, degree in hand. *Oblivious*, he was naked, out in public. Just like the *Naked Emperor*—no one could check. He jumped up out the dream, in a cold sweat!

Hours had passed, and the sun had set. Mad calls were missed. Mes'siyah took a shit, then showered, made himself a big sandwich, then Face-timed Ivory.

"Hello…" she said without a welcoming smile.

"Suppp?" Mes'siyah said.

"What do you want?" she asked, arrogantly. She still had an attitude about the stunt he pulled on her.

"What's all that about?"

"Because, you disrespectful. I don't know what you used to, but I'm not okay with all that. I have morals."

"You still mad?"

"I'm not over it. You're disrespectful."

"I want to move on, pass that."

"Why, so you can do it again? That was weird, man! Are you that full of yourself?"

Mes'siyah took a bite from his sandwich as he sat at the island, searching for the right words.

Ivory watched him, thinking of how attractive he was. The height, the ink on his skin, the waves, the beard, the smile. But she also saw conceit, narcissism, and unpredictability.

Then he said, "That will never happen again. You deserve better than me. My word."

And, there was the charm.

"What made you call me?"

Mes'siyah declined to tell her he was dreaming about her. He said, "You wasn't gonna call me."

"Was I supposed to? After you Face-timed me and had a chick sucking you off???"

"I wish it was you sucking me off," he replied, staring right into her eyes.

Penelope was just around the corner, listening and watching intently, and in disbelief. She was certain it would be her and Mes'siyah that night. She had even slipped into something super sexy from Rihanna's new fashion line.

Simpering, Ivory said, "Really? Only me, huh?"

"Clearly..."

BOOG DENIRO

"You ain't playing games with me, is you?"
"No more games."
"Well, maybe I should take my shirt off, like you,"
Ivory suggested.
"Why not???"
And, she did.
Penelope was vexed.

CHAPTER NINE

JUNE 21, 2016
FRIDAY NIGHT OUT

After 20-plus years in the clink, Charleston "Smally G" Smallwood was finally a free man. The Commissioner of the Pennsylvania parole board thought Smally G had been rehabilitated, and could be a productive member of society upon his release.

Smally G was leaving behind a few good men, but so much lied ahead of him. He just so happened to be released on the very same day that Angel King let the world know the she and Bish were expecting their third child...*finally*.

Smally G watched as thousands of social media friends and followers *commented*, *liked*, or *retweeted* the news. Angel's pages was public, so anyone could look in. Facebook, Instagram, Snapchat, Twitter. And, Smally G had no problem navigating his fancy phone. He'd been using it for more than a year now, tracking his ex-lover, and his ex-homie...

So, it should've been no surprise that he knew the Kings would be in New York celebrating the conception of their last child.

Smally G wasn't much younger than Bish, however

he looked a lot more youthful than his old crony. *Prison had preserved him.* So, instead of telling women he was going on 43-years old, he passed himself off easily as thirty, and with no mention of his time in prison whatsoever.

$ $ $

Angel wore an all white pants suit, red Christian Louboutin pumps with chrome spikes, flawless ice on her neck, wrist and ankle. Her makeup, hair, eyebrows and lashes were all done in her old Bronx neighborhood, during a day spent with her precious Rubi.

Bish wore all white too, as did their 21-year-old and their 18-year-old. Photos were taken, reporters and bloggers used their press passes to get firsthand scoop at the Manhattan venue. Angel hoped her baby-shower would be as mesmerizing as the dinner party she planned for 250 guests.

Bish was able to get Angel's mother and sister to stop by. And Angel was so happy to see them.

As things were winding down—Mes'siyah and the gang were on their way back to Philly, and Rubi and her girl crew were nowhere in sight—Smally G slid up on Bish and Angel's table. The cozy couple were alone, giddy, and just enjoying each other's company like two love-birds in the initial stages of their romance.

"Well, well, well," Smally G began.

Bish looked up, the familiar undertone resonating immediately. Angel gasped, glaring from Smally G to her husband, in total surprise. The hand with her huge wedding ring reached for Bish's right hand.

Smally G was donned in a red two-piece suit, white button down, white high top Prada sneakers, and a diamond in each earlobe. His wavy hair was jet black, as was his goatee. The brother was sharp.

Bish noticed Smally G's younger brother, Mar, ambling aimlessly with a cocktail in hand, and said, "Welcome home, brother."

"Yes, welcome home," Angel followed up with. It marked the first time she'd seen him in decades, and certainly as Mrs. Bishop King.

"Welcome, my ass..." Smally G mouthed loud enough that only the Kings could hear him.

Bish changed his pitch from peaceful to powerful, and said, "What are you doing here???" His lips were tight, and his teeth were clenched.

Smally G sat, grabbed a napkin, opened it up, sat it in his lap, all proper and whatnot. He picked up a fork and took a piece of grilled lobster from Bish's plate.

Whispers was just a table away with his lady, peeping the whole exchange. He knew Smally G too, and very well. He knew this day would come. But not in the city that never sleeps. His lady of twenty-five years whispered, "Is that Charleston?"

Whispers simply nodded.

Smally G expressed his approval for the food, "*Delicious.*" He took a few more bites as Bish stared through tight eyes. While crossing his leg, right over left, Smally G said, "*Angel Face.* Long time no see. And I mean, you still look the same. You giving these young girls hell I bet..."

You look exactly the same too, Angel thought as she maintained her composure and that grip on Bish's hand.

As Whispers neared, Smally G said, "Yeah, been about twenty-one years. Ain't dat right, Whispers?"

"Sounds about right," Whispers replied, slipping his hands into the pockets of his fitted black slacks.

"When I left you was buying a half, and I was buying a whole one. I hear you way pass that now, Bish. I hear, you running the city," Smally G said, looking around as unsuspecting friends and family danced and chatted.

"Don't believe everything you hear," Bish said.

"And you just leave a nigga like me in the gutter," Smally G said, loosening the white tie around his neck and shaking his head at the same time.

"Whispers, you gave him that?" Bish asked.

"Without a doubt," Whispers assured in his raspy, weathered voice.

Bish said, "A half million. That's a pricy ass *gutter*."

"Oh, I see, Whispers is doing all the dirty work," Smally G said, still smirking. He was truly enjoying himself.

From a short distance, and farther than his liking, Mar

was enamored by his brother going at the big time boss. After all the phone calls about how they were going to take over, it felt good that it was all about to come to fruition.

Angel didn't like what she'd just heard. When a half million dollars are moved, she wanted to know. She was just as intricate in their success as Bish was.

"What is your whole thing? Why are you in New York? Like, what's up? You should be somewhere getting some pussy," Bish told Smally G without raising his voice.

Smally G burst out into a hysterical cackle that got the attention of a few guests. "I was getting pussy while I was behind the wall, nigga," he said, just loud enough for those at the table to hear. "And don't forget, I was busting that open,"—he pointed at Angel—"before you went behind my back and took my bitch."

Bish and Angel both knew that was coming. So, neither was really surprised he only saw Angel as a *possession*. And Whispers knew the backstory as well.

Bish said, "Angel had never been yours, *and she has always been mine*."

Smally G went on to say, "I guess my twenty-plus days with her will never trump your twenty-plus years? But, what I won't look pass is you leaving me in the lion's den."

"So what are you saying?" Bish snapped, rising from his seat. He towered over Smally G by about a half foot.

As if he wasn't just released the day before, Smally G snatched a firearm from his waist so fast no one seen it coming. He had it trained on Bish beneath the table.

Bish pulled out as well, wondering *why didn't we put metal detectors at the door???* Everything was in jeopardy now.

"Try me," Smally G seethed, "I'll turn your face into a daiquiri, right here, right now, at ya dinner party. Or, *we can play nice.*"

Angel had maneuvered her tiny pistol from out her purse without Smally G taking notice, and had it trained on Smally G. But Mar *had* peeped her, and said, "Think about the baby you're carrying, Mrs. King..."

Whispers slipped between the two heated men, and Bish reclaimed his seat. Smally lowered his weapon as his heart rate began to slow down. The security detail were better shooters, quicker shots, and all over everything. That made Angel relax, but she would never forget how that pudgy fat bastard had just told her to *think about the baby you're carrying Mrs. King.* She knew their lives would never be the same, and at the same time was glad the press had left before the scene.

Smally G wanted everything Bish had acquired in his absence. He even wanted Angel back—*that's how fine she was.*

"Maybe I should've took that public defender you took..." Smally said, shaking his head.

"Fuck out of here, Smally..." Bish countered.

"Oh, he's district attorney now, ain't that right, Whispers?" Smally said, unbuttoning his sports jacket.

Angel was forced to recall the *indecent proposal* play she had encountered with Sydney Manning...

As Smally G and Mar made their way to the exit, he turned back and said, "You fucked my sister too. I know it!"

Angel said, "You fucked his sister?"

"I don't know what she told him. But it's not true. I haven't been with another woman since the day I fell in love with you. And that is the honest to God truth."

"You gave him five hundred grand?"

"In all small bills," Bish told her, as their eyes locked.

Angel said, "Take care of that and get our money back form that ungrateful bastard."

Smally G had traveled to New York three cars deep, and was trying to get back to Philly· where he was comfortable at. Inside the car he was riding in, his brother Mar asked, "That nigga gave you a half mill?"

"So what if he did?" Smally G shot back, while texting with his homie who was still in prison. He couldn't help but tell the fellas how he showed up the legendary Bishop King.

"Because, then all this is unnecessary. Unless, of course, it's about Angel King?"

Smally G snarled at his brother, who was just ten when Smally G left the streets. His brother was his lifeline while he was inside, but he was free now. And, the man calling the shots. "The next time you question me about mines, you gonna have to show me that you can rumble, youngin'!"

Mar sucked his teeth.

"Did I make myself clear?" Smally G asked over an incoming call.

Yeah, it's about that bitch, Mar believed. And he wasn't about to let Smally G know he knew, so he said, "I got you, big brah."

LATER THAT NIGHT, while on their company copter heading back to Philadelphia, Angel and Bish didn't speak much. Bish was consulting with some of his young execs under KING ENTERPRISES about upcoming events on the music side of things, and buildings needing rehabbed. Angel on the other hand, was looking at old images from their yester years and remembering how they'd gotten so far.

Angel Face...that's what she was going by when she thought she was going to be a superstar in the rap industry. It was 1995, the golden era for street entrepreneurs and indie rap labels. Her lyrics were dope, her delivery was bananas, and she had heads bopping. But she wasn't Li'l Kim, or Foxy Brown. She didn't have a male counterpart already charting, and willing to share the stage with her. But her skills had the ability to put her in the right places at the right time sometime..

URBAN ROYALTY

By the beginning of 1996 she found herself being courted by young hustlers. And she wound up preggers. Uncertain about the paternity, she lost a lot of sleep. She had been with Smally G and King Bish in the same week. She had made love to Bish, and just days before, she'd granted Smally G's wishes to taste her and make her cummm.

Bish's advances weren't just sexual, they were of genuine interest. He saw past her beauty, style and charisma. He thought Angel's view of the streets and perception of reality was rather unique, mirrored his quite a bit, and just enjoyed listening to her speak.

Smally G was smooth and flashy, things a young lady could find admirable about a dude, but she knew she was just a piece of meat to a man like him.

*A Jay-Z lyric came to mind—"...**girls in the projects wouldn't fuck us, said we talk too much...**"*

That's how she met the Philly duo...not fucking with dudes in her neighborhood.

Right after Bish snuck her out to Philly, Smally G oblivious to the power move, the Market Street murder happened.

Bishop King's face was all over the news, right next to Charleston Smallwood's.

The only two possible fathers of her baby were facing life in prison. But her connection was to Bish. In a new city, with no friends, an empty apartment, she knew she had to do whatever it took to bring Bish home. That's

97

when she first met Sydney Manning. He reminded her of Brad Pitt, upon first meeting him. He spoke flowingly about his civic duties as a Public Defender, then told Angel he had only tried one other murder case before that one.

Angel recalled being very distraught. She recalled trying to move some of the work Bish had left behind. Then on one meeting with Sydney Manning, she wasn't showing yet, but knew she would be any day now, he asked her for one night alone with her. And that if she agreed, he would dedicate every resource he had to clearing Bish of all charges.

"Promise," Angel demanded.

Sydney Manning promised.

They went out to Harrisburg, Pennsylvania, where no one knew them, and the thirty-year old attorney courted the 18-year old soon-to-be-mom.

At the hotel, she gave him head, they had intercourse, he ate her pussy and her asshole, he bathed her, then she fell asleep. That happened again, and again while Bish languished in prison. And, then Bish was home.

Manning had kept his word, and he never contacted her again...

In her eyes, Angel had done what she had to do to secure her future, and had no regrets about it.

CHAPTER TEN

JUNE 29, 2016
SATURDAY 11PM

Outside of Ridge Capitol, Rubi and her girls exited their vehicles and enjoyed the black summer night. It was dark out, but the lights were bright. Street lights, and headlights illuminated the scene.

A white Jaguar honked the horn at them. The 2016 model was breathtaking, big and boss like, looking like luxury. And all four of them took a peek to see who the driver was. The hazard lights come on, and out hopped a muscular fellow, about 180 lbs, his diamonds lighting it up. The swag in his strut, and the pep in his step, exuded confidence. The white *shelltoe* Adidas were new. The white PRP's fit properly. The white and crème Louis Vuitton belt held the gun on his hip close. The fitted white LV Tee allowed his chain to swing, and his Rolex to attract attention. Anyone looking could tell he worked out faithfully, and took good care of his teeth and skin. He was standing about 5'9", and his chocolate skin shone in the night. He walked up to the girls, all his attention on Rubi whom did not look eighteen that night.

Rubi had on a hot pink romper with elastic in the hem

that gripped her calves, showing off her ankles and feet. The fabric was so soft, Rubi's ass just wiggled with each step she took in her high price stilettos. And that day she decided not to wear a bra, so her tits looked lush with the thick nipples penetrating the top part of the romper. She would be nineteen in a few weeks, but appeared to be in her prime.

The chocolate brother licked his lips, took Rubi's hand into his, and said, "What's up, *superstar*?"

Another groupie, she wanted to think, but he resembled a superstar too. And his voice was deep and rugged, and smooth and intoxicating, and made Rubi's girls a bit envious he didn't speak to them. Goosebumps formed on Rubi's biceps and forearms. *Trap God is cute, but this brother is gorgeous*, she said to herself.

She further observed him from his wavy hair to his sneakers, and said, "Just out, me and *my gurls*."

"And your name is?"

"Rubi..."

"I need your number, Rubi," he said, staring into her eyes. His face was so close to Rubi's, she could smell the Big Red gum on his breath.

She chortled, looking to her girls for approval. While she was doing that, Trap God's small entourage drove by in their small fleet of cars. The guy Mes'siyah had shot in the shoulder was riding shotgun with Trap God, bobbing his head to something by Meek Mill.

Rubi's girl, Imani, was dressed to impressed, had spent her entire allowance to do it too, and made eye contact with one of the main players in the Trap God's outfit. Her parent's held her down, so long as she stayed in college, but she was still in search of a sponsor. Imani's parent's weren't kingpins, they weren't *urban royalty*, they were hardworking middle class folk.

After logging her number in the guy's iPhone, Rubi said, "And who's gonna be calling me?"

"Oh, I'm Charlie."

"And how old are you, Charlie?"

He smiled again, flashing his freshly whitened teeth, and said, "I'll be thirty in a few weeks."

Twenty-nine, thought Rubi, pondering was that too old. *He's got me by ten years.*

"And how *young* are you?" he asked Rubi.

"I be twenty-one,"—she paused—"in a few weeks."

She wasn't a good liar, and dude picked up on that quick. But it didn't matter. Two liars deserved each other.

"What's your sign?" Rubi asked him.

"Cancer," he proudly announced.

"Me too!" Rubi revealed.

She was intrigued on many levels. In some ways he reminded her of Mes'siyah. He didn't have a big fluffy beard, or the tattoos, or the height, but everything else was there. She thought maybe Mes'siyah would identify with dude, and finally accept a man she was show-

101

interest in. She was in a daze, and didn't even feel Charlie's lips on her forehead.

"I gotta go. But I'll be in touch." And with that, Charlie's driver was gone.

The girls went into the club and shut it down for a couple hours. Guys were ogling, gawking, and they loved the attention.

Rubi had an early breakfast with Trap God at a local diner around three that morning, but she was thinking about Charlie's *smooth ass* the whole time. Imani locked in her newest sponsor, as they slid off together.

THE NEXT MORNING, Rubi showered, slipped into some shorts and a cute Tee, so she could just lounge around the mansion in comfort. Maybe Charlie would call??? Maybe he was at church??? Maybe they could spend their birthdays together???

It was around 10:00 AM when Rubi smelled the aroma of French toast. She headed towards the wonderful scent, singing a tune by Trey Songz.

Meanwhile, on the other side of the residence, Mes'siyah was just rising from slumber too. He had partied hard the night before too, out in New York with Mally Gz and his Bronx crew.

"Good morning, Mes'siyah," a high yellow house-keeper said, as she dusted a vase by the TV room.

"Morning to you too, Bev," Mes'siyah shot back.

"Will you be having breakfast with the family?"

"No. Won't even be here that long."

"Okay," Beverly said, as Mes'siyah made his way to the vault. He had picked up a grip of cash from Mally Gz while in New York, most of which belonged to his parents. After putting his cut up, he headed to Bish's office, taking the secret door, which he just found out his mother had been traveling through too lately. The other night he heard them in there *fucking*.

His phone rang. It was Sacari.

"Yo, Bro," Mes'siyah said, entering the secret door.

"I'm ready," Sacari replied.

"Alright, I'm on my way."

Mes'siyah was about to hang up, when Sacari said, "Tell Rubi to keep her lil ass out Capitol Ridge. All the dope boys was all over her lil crew, Bro."

"Clearly." Mes'siyah put the cash where it belonged, then unzipped the duffels. "Thanks, Bro."

"See you when you get here."

"Clearly." Mes'siyah hung up. He had corrupted Sacari's little brother, but he wanted to keep his little sister *pure*.

Two at a time, Mes'siyah tossed kilos into three duffels, then stuffed the bags into the trunk of the Bentley. Once done, he snickered, walking back into the mansion, and towards his family whom were congregating though in their own worlds.

Uneasy, Bish was reading the newspaper while picking at his food. Angel was checking out an article in Essence magazine about breast feeding, while sipping a cold glass of orange juice. Fucking up some scrambled eggs and French toast, Rubi was doing some online shopping.

"Old head…"

"Young boy…"

"Momma…"

"My Mes'siyah…" Angel replied, smiling at him.

Rubi looked up, wondering why she wasn't greeted, only to see a right hand coming at her.

Swattt!

The sound made the smack seem much worse than it really was. Rubi had dipped that shit and slid down off the high sitting stool, falling on her ass.

Bish quickly rose from his thoughts in disbelief, asking, "Yo, young boy, fuck is you doing?"

Angel grabbed Bish's hand, and shook her head *no*. She tapped his hand, and he sat back down as if he were trained.

Mes'siyah leaned down and swung an open hand at Rubi's pretty face again, connecting a bit more flush that time. And it dazed Rubi. She was seeing stars.

He grabbed her by her long lustrous hair, pulling her to the center of the ground floor. "You think it's a game? Shit ain't a game, lil girl!"

Rubi screamed, "Daddy!"

Bish couldn't watch. He felt weak, docile, unmanly, and helpless, and couldn't believe Angel was actually holding him back.

Once Mes'siyah got Rubi where he wanted her, he began to site her disrespect. "I told you to stay out the city, you still go there. I tell you to stay out the clubs, you all up in the clubs. I tell you to keep them niggas out ya face, they all up in ya grill. You just don't get it. Until ya ass get kidnapped, and they send a ransom note. Or, you get touched for some foul shit ya family did."

Angel whispered to Bish, "That's why you let it play out, daddy."

Mes'siyah continued, "And when those things happen, Daddy gonna blame me. Mommy gonna want me to get out there in those streets and bring ya ass back to the King compound."

Rubi wept senselessly, and until Mes'siyah released her from his grasp. She got up and rolled her eyes at Angel. She turned her nose up at Bish. The maids and the cooks got back to work, fearing Rubi's wrath.

Bish felt like shit, while Angel moved on to an article in the Philadelphia Daily News about a new DA looking to come in and clean the office up.

When Angel felt Bish peering down on her with strained eyes, she looked up and said, "She's been lying to us the entire time about where she's been going when she leaves here. And she's too big for us to be beating her."

"Beating her?" Bish snapped. "The damn girl will be nineteen in a few weeks. She's *grown!*"

"Still need checks and balances in her life," Angel countered. "And she's under our roof."

"Angel, do me a favor," Bish asked.

"Anything for you, my king," Angel said, sitting the newspaper down on the island top, giving Bish here undivided attention.

Without reservation, Bish said, "Shut the fuck up!"

Before Angel could say or do anything in response, Bish went on saying, "You posting all our business on social media is how the fuck Smally knew we were in New York. We all gots to tighten the fuck up!" And with that, he left her sitting alone, almost brushing shoulder's with Mes'siyah who was in shock that his father had spoken to his mother in that fashion.

Angel dropped her head, shut her eyes, and prayed. She prayed for her family's safety and protection, for a healthy full term pregnancy, and that this trying time wouldn't put a strain on her marriage.

Deep down, she knew things were about to take a turn for the worse.

Silent, and slowly, Mes'siyah stalked out...shaking his head. In his mind, this was all Rubi's fault. Not the lifestyle their parents perpetuated, and brought them up in.

CHAPTER ELEVEN

JULY 3, 2016
WEDNESDAY, 1PM

Rubi could feel a helicopter approaching minutes before anyone else heard the whack of rotors.

She was poolside, sunbathing, and pondering her next move. *There is no way Mes'siyah is going to get away with slapping me down and dragging me by my freaking hair last Sunday, while my parents, Penelope and the rest of the help stood by watching.*

In her hand was her phone, and it was at that moment that she learned her mother had premiered No.3 on the Instagram Luxe List for leading entrepreneurs in urban culture. Angel was widely recognized as the face of King Enterprises. The photo the blogger used for the piece featured Angel Ross-King standing with her best friend and fashion designer Brook Burnside.

Angel didn't consider herself a celeb, she thought of herself as more of a hustler. But she never turned down the opportunity to build on the brand.

It was times like this that made Rubi proud to be Angel's daughter. Made her want to be just like her mother. Without another thought, she shared the post on her social media.

As she was interacting with followers, not far away the copter was landing on the compound's helipad.

Angel could see Rubi from the distance as she hopped down out of the helicopter. Brook was not far behind Angel, and talking on her phone.

"Rubi," Angel said, startling her daughter.

Rubi removed her shades and looked up.

Angel said, "I was thinking, Brook's in town, and you know your brother is having that event; maybe we could go together…"

"Congratulations on the making the Luxe List again this year. But, I think I'll pass."

"Thank you. But I don't need them to validate me. I want you to reconsider too." She kissed Rubi's shiny forehead, then added, "It'll be fun."

"It looked like you were having fun watching your son abuse me," Rubi shot bac, stunning Angel.

If not now, than when?, Angel thought while peering down on her daughter who reminded her so much of herself when she was younger.

Brook's heels could be heard click-clacking in the distance. So Angel leaned in and said, "I'm sorry things went the way they did. But, Mes'siyah is your brother, and he loves you as we all do, and he was just trying protect you from yourself. Sometimes it's not pretty."

"Hi, Rubi!" Brook shouted, stuffing her phone back into her oversized bag.

Angel met Brook when she was about 28-years old,

and spending a lot of time at the headquarters for *Dir'Me* Clothing. Brook was an intern for the brand, with a keen eye for fashion and the newest *it* thing. She went on to become a creative director with *Dir'Me*, and one of Angel's closest friends in the process. They vacationed together once a year, shared secrets, voiced concerns, and even complaints. A better job opportunity opened up for Brook in Los Angeles, and since Angel was in the process of relocating to California, they'd been kicking it heavy. Which was why Brook was on the east coast visiting.

"Auntie Brook!" Rubi shouted back.

The two embraced while Angel watched, and hoping her daughter would reconsider.

"So, did your mom tell you I want us to all hang out?" Brook asked.

"Did my mom tell you she let Mes'siyah put his hands on me...*without interjecting*?"

"Rubi," Angel said, intervening. "I don't think that is open for discussion at the present moment. And I believe that is a mischaracterization of the facts."

"Mom, Auntie Brook, have fun..." With that, Rubi got up and went into the house.

LATER THAT EVENING, luxurious giggles filled Rubi's room as she admired her image and style in the huge mirror, her phone to her ear. She grabbed her oversized designer bag off the chair. "Charlie, yes, I'm coming. I'm leaving in a minute," Rubi assured, while *approving* of what she saw in the mirror. She wore a curve hugging greenish floral silk jumper by *Dir'Me*. A split came down the sides, right over her thighs and down to her ankles. The waistline came across the abdomen, while the collar hugged her neck. The neckline plunged to her navel showing off her new belly-button piercing. She was also braless, *side-boob showing*. There was very little left to the imagination. *Even her Gucci stilettos showed most of her feet.*

"Can't wait to see you," Charlie said in this deep and alluring voice that did something to Rubi.

She said, "Don't tell me, show me…"

"Say that again," Charlie shot back, grinning.

Rubi repeated herself, loud and clear, and Charlie said, "Say lessssss."

That warmed her up even more. So much that she hadn't even noticed Penelope slip into her bedroom.

Penelope just listened for a moment, then slipped around to where she was standing right before Rubi, admiring the large gold and VVS diamond hoop earrings in Rubi's ears. Penelope then sized up the heart shaped ruby locket hanging from the skinny Cuban link on Rubi's neck. Then she touched Rubi's gold woman's Rolex.

Rubi thought nothing of it. She actually liked Penelope. When she hung up with Charlie, she said, "What's up, Penelope?"

"*You*," Penelope told the young stunner. "Look like you're going out to have some fun."

"I am," Rubi said. "And you should too. Waiting around here for my brother to finally realize you are *dope* is getting played out."

"WOW. That was cold, Rubi."

"You think I don't know what you two be sneaking around here doing?"

Penelope said, "I am crazy about him."

Without even considering what Penelope had just said, Rubi told her, "If he ever puts his hands on me again—"

"Rubi, he loves you, he just has a fucked way of showing it," she said cutting Rubi off.

"Just like he loves you, but has a fucked up way of showing it?" Rubi countered.

Penelope switched the topic. "So, who's this guy that got you grinning from ear to rear, Rubi?"

"His name is Charlie. He's a boss, just like my dad and my brother, and he's not on no young boy shit."

"Nice," Penelope cooed.

"He works out, he has this voice that is deep and dark like the chocolate brother he is…"

"Where's he from?"

"I don't know yet."

"What does he do?"

"I don't know yet."

"How'd you meet him?"

"He chose me out of all my girls. I wasn't even the baddest that night. Imani looked way better than me."

All of this seemed odd to Penelope. And she figured she could use the information to get back in Mes'siyah's good graces.

$ $ $

BISHOP, 7:20 PM...

Bish walked into the master bed. His white Jimmy Choo tennis sneakers ambled across the marble floor. The power thrust of shower water could be heard, and in his smooth stride, he followed the steam. Inside the bathroom, he said, "If I wasn't already dressed, I'd join you."

Angel slid the glass door ajar, and said, "I would like you to join me, so I can make up for my mishaps. I was out of pocket. And I get more pleasure out of admitting my faults than I would downplaying it."

"What did you have in mind?" Bish asked with his head cocked to the side, sizing his lovely wife up.

"I wanna put the whole thing in my mouth..." She said that with passion. "Feel you in the back of my throat. It'll only take me a minute to make you cumm in my mouth."

"Rain check," Bish said, then added, "Something important has come up.

"I got you, lover…" she said, assuringly.

And Bish was cool with that. After all those years, he was still in love with Angel, and no regrets about taking her from Smally G.

"I;ma bust that thang open tonight after that."

"I know that's right," Angel said, then shut the glass door and finished showering.

Bish left, went to the bookshelf, pushed a tiny button. On a shelf below, just below the one containing his business books, a secret latch fell. Inside the secret compartment that had been there since the kids were young, sat two chrome gats with the cream marble handles. Next to them were four extended clips and a Louis Vuitton shoulder holster. He slipped in the clips, holstered the pistols, and proceeded to close the secret pistol box. In the full length mirror he was checking himself out in, he witnessed Angel approaching without the shower cap, and passing a towel over her exfoliated skin.

"I can't wait till tonight. I need some now," Angel whined.

Before Bish could reply, Whispers was calling. He as out front. "Later," he reasserted.

"Okay…" she giggled like a flirtatious minx about to get hit from behind by new boyfriend for the first time.

Bish left her and took off. Angel could always tell when her king was on a mission. She knew Bish was still working on *bringin' that $500,000 back to momma.*

Bish had been in the city every night since that run-in with Smally G in the fashion capitol. He wanted to finish him, find a hole, and bury him. But, Smally G was one step ahead of Bish.

When Bish came down the front steps of the mansion, Rubi was out front. Almost as if she was waiting on her father. "How you feeling?" he immediately asked upon seeing her. He thought she may've still been a bit traumatized from the checking Mes'siyah had put on her. So he had been a little extra attentive. Extra spending money, surprise bouquets, even put new rims on her Porsche truck.

"I want to go to Mes'siyah's block party. Can I go? I already missed Young Sheemi's performance."

He looked his daughter up and down and said, "You already look like you're going." He kissed her on her forehead and added, "Be good."

Even if he had said *no*, she was going. There was no way she was missing the opportunity to link up with Charlie. "Thank you, daddy! Can I have Young Sheemi at my nineteenth birthday party?"

"Sure, babygirl," he said, then hit his boss stride, gliding pass the guard dogs roaming.

Whispers was behind the wheel of the Rolls Royce, hands snug in black leather gloves, gripping the steering wheel. "My man," he said.

"He's there?" Bish asked, too slipping his paws into some black leather gloves.

114

Whispers said, "Twenty minutes ago he was. Don't see why he wouldn't be now."

"Let's make this quick…"

Not long after Bish said that, they were there.

"Hey, Mrs. June," Bish greeted, showing off his remarkably white and disciplined teeth.

"Bishop King, the entrepreneur, the myth, the legend. What brings you out to Cherry Hill this evening?" Smally G's mother replied, bugging Bish. "You just missed Charleston," she added, about to shut the screen door when she noticed Whispers squeezing inside too.

"Them bills still paying themselves?" Bish asked, chuckling and accepting her embrace.

"Sure is," Mrs. June replied, extending her arms for Whispers.

Bish had paid Smally G's mother's bills for the better part of Smally G's lengthy incarceration. *Smally G didn't know that.* And Bish wanted it that way; quiet as kept. Not for the world to know. Because Smally G would've told everyone; with his spin on it. Like, he was extorting the Kings.

"By chance, did he say where he was going?" Bish asked, unable to look the woman in her aging eyes.

"He said something about going to the block party in the southwest. The old neighborhood," she revealed, shrugging her withering shoulders, palms to the sky, and approaching her rocking chair.

"Block party, hmm?" Bish quizzed, unable to contain

the grin taking hold of his face. She was talking about the Block Party Mes'siyah had put on with Ms. Gloria from the old neighborhood.

"I think..." she added, leaning back in her seat.

Bish opened the fridge, and helped himself to a bottle of apple juice.

Mrs. June noticed that both men were wearing gloves, midsummer, and she squinted, bringing about the crowfeet in the corners of her eyes. "Now that I think about it, he might be with his new girlfriend."

As he shut the refrigerator door, Bish shook the bottle for premium flavor. He opened it and wet his whistler, then said, "Ice cold. It's in my veins."

While Mrs. June was watching Bish, Whispers whipped out the piano wire from his Levi's jeans pocket, and lifted the woman from her seat by her neck. He held the wire to her throat until she had been deprived enough oxygen then set her back in her rocking chair. He turned her head towards the jumbo flat screen. A Tyler Perry movie was on.

"Ice cold," Bish said one more time as the duo shut the wooden and screen doors behind them. "It's a good thing I moved her way out here a couple years ago when we realized Smally was getting short."

"Easy to get in, easy to get out," Whispers said, agreeing with his crime partner. They slipped into a jet black Honda Accord coupe.

"Thaila made sure the deed for the house would be

traced back to Mar's corny ass, and not us," Bish mentioned, taking his gloves off.

Within minutes, Whispers had them to the Rolls Royce, and at the Block Party. The two comrades walked up 57th Street and Wallace, to 58th Street. Local politicians from both sides of the party line were out on display, as a camera crew with the local news captured it all. The Mayor noticed Bish and said, "Bishop King, entrepreneur, the man, the myth..."

That spooked the shit out of Bish. Smally G's mother had said something almost identical.

"Are you okay? Did I say something wrong?" the Mayor asked.

"Mayor, it's good to see you again...and I'm fine."

"You looked spooked," the Mayor went on saying.

While Bish was shaking hands with the largest politician in the city, his son was a block away smoking some OG Kush. Sacari was by Mes'siyah's side wondering if his friend was losing his mind. Right before the block party they were planning a kidnapping. Another hustler was trying to part ways with Mes'siyah. Mes'siyah didn't see those guys as his partners, he saw them as his possessions. At least that's the way Sacari was beginning to see things.

When the blunt was done, they headed towards the barricaded part of the neighborhood, and there Mes'siyah noticed his father talking to some State Representatives. He also peeped Ivory Manning.

"Ivory with two of her closest girlfriends," Mes'siyah muttered. They young women were enjoying food and music, paper plates in their hands.

Mes'siyah lusted for a minute or two as Ivory was dressed to the nines. Her toes, nails, and hair was done immaculately.

Alone, Mes'siyah approached Bish, hand extended. He said, "Father."

"Son…"

They smiled at each other, almost in this knowing way, like they spoke their own language, and Bish said, "You did a good job in a week's notice, young boy."

Blushing, Mes'siyah said, "I am my father's son."

Bish then introduced his prodigal son to the power players fiending to be in his presence. With the elections looming, the criminal justice reform thing pushing to the forefront of politics, no one was donating more money to campaigns than Bishop King.

The Mayor said, "You set this up, young man?"

Like a young kid, innocent to the world, Mes'siyah said, "Yes, sir, I did."

"What a way to celebrate Independence," the Mayor said, then posed in a picture with the Kings, father and son, for the optics.

Bish whispered to Mes'siyah, "Your sister is here, and I gave her permission to be here, so be nice. Do I make myself clear?"

"Clearly…" Mes'siyah reluctantly replied.

CHAPTER TWELVE

SAME DAY, 8:44 PM

Rubi noticed Mar leaned back on the hood of a triple black Hell Cat, parked about five vehicles from the corner of 58th Street. Cheesing, Rubi parked, got out and said, "You as black as the night…"

"Lil sis. Why don't you bring the light skinned chick with you next time?"

"Which one? We all light skin, except my best friend."

"The one with the tats."

"Imani," Rubi said. "She should be here. We were texting while I was on my way." As soon as she said that, the driver's side door of the Hell Cat popped open. After an intense gaze, Rubi got into the passenger side and saw smoke coming from Charlie's curled lips.

"Baby girl," he said, smiling.

"Hey, Charlie…"

"My cutie," he replied, checking out this fresh piece of ass. While in the joint, he used to dream about moments like this one. Just looking at Rubi was making his manhood stretch out the front of his jeans. He was well endowed too. So Rubi noticed.

"That don't smell like weed," Rubi noticed and said.

119

"They call this *toochie*."

"Never heard of it," Rubi said, smacking her lips and eyeing Charlie fine and fly ass down.

"Wanna see what it's hitting for?"

"My brother told me...don't smoke nothing I didn't roll, or didn't see get rolled."

The synthetic weed was beginning to take its effect on Charlie. He was feeling it. *And feeling Rubi.* He turned the music on, and Jeremih sang:

....If it look this good ....I wonder how it taste... ...Baby if I touch yo body ...hear you scream my name....

THE 5 SENSES, that's what he had booming from the speakers as he sand along. And Rubi giggled because she thought that was *so* cute.

Charlie sat his Backwood down in the ashtray, then reached over Rubi's right shoulder and began unzipping her jumper.

Rubi looked at him like he was crazy, and said, "What are you doing?"

"I'm not a kid, Rubi. I say what I want, and as a man, I get what I want. And I wanna fuck you so bad. But not before I taste it," he told her while staring her dead in her eyes. He was also pulling the top portion of her jumper down over her shoulders as he expressed his desires.

"Charlie," Rubi said, covering her luscious brown sugar nipples with her hands.

"Damn, girl…"

"Charlie, all these people are out here."

"What you think the tint is for, Rubi King?" he told her.

"I never told you my last name…"

He grabbed her thick thighs, pulling them towards him. He yanked down her silk jumper even more. And to balance herself, Rubi released her juicy jiggling breasts. He pulled the jumper down to her ankles, and seen her flesh colored g-string. The front was lace and shaped like a butterfly. It covered her pelvic area.

"I can't believe this…" Rubi mouthed, one elbow on the door panel, the other on Charlie's husky trap muscle doing a balancing act.

He licked his lips like a wildcat, grabbed hold of the elastic on her g-string and snatched it down over her hips and knees in one swift motion.

"Charlie…" Rubi panted at his overt aggression.

His head dipped low and she felt his tongue between the first two toes on her left foot. She felt kisses on her ankles and shins. She could feel his lips traveling up her thighs, then at her inner thighs closest to her vagina.

She had totally forgot the advance was unwanted, and reminded herself that she liked this man so much that he was the first thing on her mind when she woke up.

Charlie's mouth made its way to those brown sugar nipples and he sucked them feverishly. His hungry mouth didn't leave one portion of her juicy tits unlicked.

Rubi was breathing in an unfamiliar pattern, as she panted, *"Charlie..."*

He pushed her bowlegs up and towards her chest, had her favorite shoes up near her gold and diamond hoop earrings. He locked eyes with her, then opened her legs wider and dipped his head low.

"Ohhh Charlie..." Rubi cooed. She could feel his thick tongue lap at her outer labia, then pelt across her clit. She had one of those vaginas with the pouty pussy lips, neatly trimmed, and Charlie could not believe his luck. No other man had ever given her kisses like that down low. Nor had she ever experienced an orgasm prior to that night. It was like her first puff of kush.

Charlie began to probe the pussy with his fingers, nibble on the clit, and thumb Rubi's ass hole. He slurped, he sucked, even kissed the pussy. And Rubi went crazy. It felt so good to Rubi, she found herself pulling his head to her crotch, bucking at his mouth, whining, moaning, and calling his name.

He came up, took two more puffs of that *toochie*, blew the smoke in Rubi's pretty face and just watched as she wondered why he'd stopped.

As he's expected, Rubi said, "Don't stop." And added, "Keep going, it feels...*good*."

He went right back to finger popping her booty with two fingers, and tongue kissing her clit and inner labia. Two minutes of that, and Rubi's pussy began to squirt.

Charlie, *better known as Smally G*, allowed the juices

to flow and coat his mouth and nose, and lapped up the rest that gushed from her soul. It tasted like apple juice to him. He took her wide ass in his hands and lifted all 138 pounds of Rubi up off the leather seat so he could lick the cum that was dripping down to her ass hole.

"Your tongue is in my ass now…"

Rubi's flesh was coated in sweat, the baby hairs had risen up off her forehead and temples, and she was trying to catch her breath.

Smally G was unbuckling his Gucci belt, pulling his powerful erection from his boxer briefs. Rubi thought he was going to put the dick inside her, and braced herself for her very first time. But he didn't. Instead, Smally G stood up, head nearly out the sunroof, and put it in her face. Rubi was shocked.

The warmth, the veins, the size. It was mega hard, and he rubbed it on Rubi's chin, her jawline, her neckline, before placing the engorged head on her glossy lips.

Rubi shook her head from side to side, saying, "I'm not with all that. Sorry. But no, not yet."

"Girl, you gonna suck this dick…" Charlie barked.

Rubi refused, shoving Charlie back behind the wheel.

Smally G sucked his teeth, and stared Rubi down like she'd stolen something from him. It got quiet.

"You mad at me, Charlie?" Rubi asked, looking over the console at his hard dick.

Smally G knew what that meant. He had awakened

Rubi's sexual curiosity. He had Rubi King right where he wanted her. One day, before he exacted his revenge, he could say, "I fucked yo bitch, Bishop, and your daughter, niggah! Now what???"

As Rubi was embracing the idea that she wouldn't be putting out, and Smally G puffed while losing his erection, Angel was just getting to the block party.

Inside the G-wagon, Brook Burnside, said, "I'm serious, girl. After all these years, I thought I'd be used to it. But this negro be fucking my stomach up still."

Angel laughed, looking for parking.

"I'm tired of his long dick; I want a lil' dick nigga," Brook went on saying, making Angel cackle even more.

Angel said, "Bitch, you know you don't want that fine ass nigga running up in another chick, so if he wanna rock that thang three times a day, you gonna be with it. Don't even front, Brook."

"I'm bringing in the bread, so I should be able to determined when I want the dick, and how I want the dick, right?"

"Yeah, and *no*," Angel said, having located a parking spot on 58th Street.

"He had a bitch throwing up. I was calling *earl*."

Angel said, "You might be pregnant."

"Do not say that. Don't say that, Angel Ross-King. I'm in the process of making some real money moves."

"You're thirty-five right now. Prime time. Our babies can be raised together. And money chase us, not the other way around."

Brook checked herself out in the mirror on her makeup compact, then put it back in her MK clutch. Everything was on point, except she noticed her cute button nose was widening. *Another sign that she may be pregnant.* "Did you do your pregnancy test with Bishop present?" she asked Angel.

"All three of my pregnancies. And three times, he was as anxious to know as I was."

"I'm gonna test when I get back to L.A.," Brook said a bit excited and taking her seatbelt off. "Angel is that, Rubi?"

"Where?" asked Angel, following Brook's hazelnut eyes.

"Right there!" Brook blared. "Who is that fine ass dude with her? Zipping her up? He just smacked her on her ass, Angel! Rubi has gotten thicker than a king size snickers. *Body banging too!!! Dammnmn!*"

After tapping Rubi on that round ass, Smally G got back behind the wheel. Rubi leaned into the car just as Angel peeped her daughter's bowlegs and earrings.

Angel was speechless. Rubi would be nineteen soon. *So that's what she told Brook, to conceal her true feelings.*

"True. I started fucking when I was fourteen. I made love for the first time when I was eighteen," Brook revealed, flowingly and unabashed.

They exited the G-Wagon, two beautiful, and fierce

black women in their primes, and a lot of eyes were on them. The block was packed with young boys, established men, a few old heads, and they were all checking out Angel and Brook.

Angel watched Rubi kiss the driver of the Hell Cat passionately, and heard Rubi giggling as she and Brook crossed the street.

"Young boy, we out," Angel also heard the driver say. She watched a dude talking on a phone get into the Hell Cat. She knew she'd seen the guy before but was unable to place him.

Rubi looked up and saw her mother as Mar shut the door. The engine growled ferociously, Smally G hit the horn and peeled off, the dual exhaust pipes spitting smoke as the car busted a sharp U-turn and shot up Florence like a bat out of hell.

"Mom???" *Rubi was surprised.*

Angel didn't want to show Rubi up in front of Brook, so she pulled Rubi to the side. "You having quickies in cars now, with all these people out here?" she said, seething and looking Rubi up and down.

Rubi was confused. "Huh?"

"You pussy is soaking wet?" Angel shot directly into Rubi's right ear with her teeth clenched.

Rubi looked down, witnessing the wet spot and streaks flowing through the crotch and inner thigh part of her jumper. That's when she realized Smally G still had her g-string. She placed her handbag in front of her, held it in place with both hands. She was truly nervous, even though she was a woman now. Something like that could get her cut off from her parents' fortune, forcing her to either go to college or find a job.

"You have absolutely no respect for yourself, or this family. You could have gotten a room. What were you thinking, Rubi King???"

"*Mommmmm...*"

"I can't wait to see your father, and tell him that I know what you're doing now when you are in the city."

"*But...*"

"You make it easy for the opposition to infiltrate the kingdom when you do simple shit like this. You do know what, right? *Look at me.*"

Brook would never admit it, but she heard everything Angel had said to Rubi. She turned her head when she was the tears falling from Rubi's pretty eyes.

It had gone from Rubi's best time ever, to her worst time ever. Just that fast.

"I wasn't fucking," Rubi finally said speaking up, even though she knew her mother wouldn't believe her.

"Right. And I *wasn't* born in the Bronx, New York."

Angel strutted off in her black strapless sundress, putting space between herself and Rubi. Her stilettoes click-clacked with Brook close by, until they reached the sound stage where Bish and Mes'siyah were.

As she was kissing Bish's lips, four hands tugged at her arm. "Mrs. Angel!" Young Sheemi and Avery Trap said it at the same time when they saw Angel. She was responsible for discovering both of them.

"My two favorite musicians," Angel said, hugging each of them. "I missed the performance?"

"The first one, earlier. But, Bishop King wants us to perform again for the Mayor. So that's what we about to do when Rico Havoc is done doing his thing. Our new collabo," Avery Trap said as she swung the super long tresses of her raven wig back over her bare shoulders.

Angel forced a smile, and said, "Great." She was still reeling over Rubi's public promiscuity.

"Pictures???" a local photographer with the Philly Inquire asked.

"Yeah. Come on, baby girl," Bish said, and Angel looked back locking eyes with Rubi.

Mes'siyah had Ivory under his right arm, so she got in the pictures too. Bish was in the middle, Angel on his right, Rubi on his left. Young Sheemi and Avery Trap leaned in next to Mes'siyah and Ivory. Brook posted up by her best friend Angel, holding her stomach. Even the Mayor and a couple State Reps took part in the optics before the photographer was done snapping away.

After the last flick was taken, Angel whispered something in Bish's ear, and he said, "She what?" Bish's nostrils flared, his lips got tight, as did he eyes. He had vouched for her, gave her permission to come into the city, and she disappointed him. *He was furious*.

Mes'siyah took his palm from Ivory's plump derriere and asked Angel, "What's good? Everything cool?"

"We now know, undisputed, why my daughter loves being in Philadelphia so much, and so bad," Angel told him in a low pitch. She pulled Bish in closer. It was so low, Mes'siyah had to lean in more. *"Your* sister, and *your* daughter, likes riding boys in cars."

Brook wanted to say, *That's not completely true.* Rubi hadn't actually been caught doing anything except kissing a man. But it wasn't her place. She was a family friend, not a family member. And she felt so bad because it was she who had noticed Rubi, and pointed her out to Angel.

As that was unfolding, Young Sheemi and Avery Trap performed their new collaboration *Wild Sexy!* Avery Trap was a sultry R&B singer in her early twenties a lot of people liked to compare to Kehlani. And Young Sheemi was a young MC coming into his own from the Bronx. He could sing and he rapped, and was discovered killing it on YouTube.

Bish, Whispers, Mes'siyah and Sacari stood off to the side trying to figure out how no one had seen Smally G. They had men with a picture of Smally G on their phone screens scouring the block party looking for him for about an hour now.

As soon as the recording artists were done, they found the Kings. Angel and Brook were congratulating them when Smally G took notice of the gathering. He was in a wig full of dreads and coming fast.

Bish was saying, "I want him dead. *Tonight*. We have our best men out here. I'll put the half million back myself. Do I make myself clear???"

"Hey, Bish!"

BOCKA! BOCKA! BOCKA! BOCKA!

Not many people heard the shots, just saw some scrambling. Bish leaped atop Angel who was just a couple feet away. Mes'siyah and Sacari pulled their weapons. And, it was dark.

Avery Trap and Young Sheemi had been some of the few who heard the shots, being in such close proximity, and panicked.

The shots kept coming, and the music kept playing, disguising the popping sounds.

As Whispers and Mes'siyah hit the sidewalk... *Boom! Boom! BOOM! BOOM!*

Smally G stumbled backwards, dreads covering his face, when he noticed Rubi rushing to a bush. He stopped shooting. Sacari noticed, and took aim at the dread.

Finally, people figured out there was a gun battle going on in the vicinity.

"Oh shit, Avery Trap," Mes'siyah muttered, having noticed the young lady's white shirt stained with blood. Avery Trap had suffered multiple gunshot wounds....

Author's note

This is the first installment in the *Urban Royalty* miniseries. As you can see, success doesn't always equate to happiness. And money isn't everything. This family is divided. And it's only going to get worse.

The second installment in the series is entitled *Rubi Red, Urban Royalty 2.* With Rubi under the spell of her family's arch nemesis, and Mes'siyah still trying to save her from herself, and he not truly having direction of his own, it's sure to be jaw-dropping.

About the Author

Boog Deniro, real name TySheem Crocker, is a Bronx, New York native. He is the co-founder and CEO of S.G. Publishing.

He is also the author of *RESPECT THE STRUGGLE*, and the STREET GENERALS trilogy including: *NO SELLOUTS, NOTHING IS SACRED*, and *CAN'T STOP WON'T STOP*.

Boog Deniro also co-wrote *THE UNGODLY PASTOR* with Country McRae.

Boog Deniro is currently housed at SCI Somerset, in Pennsylvania. If his moves coincide with his intentions, he should be a free man real soon. Stay tuned!

SG PUBLISHING PRESENTS

ORDER FORM

NAME:_____#_____

ADDRESS:_____

STATE:_____ZIP_____

QTY	TITLE	PRICE
	RESPECT THE STRUGGLE	$15.00
	STREET GENERALS	$15.00
	STREET GENERALS 2	$15.00
	STREET GENERALS III	$15.00
	THE UNGODLY PASTOR	$15.00
	ANY DAY CAN BE YOUR LAST IN THE JUNGLE	$15.00
	URBAN ROYALTY	$10.00

$4.95 SHIPPING AND HANDLING

NO PERSONAL CHECKS

SEND MONEY ORDER OR INSTITUTIONAL CHECK TO:

S.G. PUSBISHING,
1610 SEDGWICK AVE
SUITE 6G
BRONX, NEW YORK, 10453

AVAILABLE ON AMAZON.COM